# The Legend of Darklore Manor

## AND OTHER TALES OF TERROR

BY JOSEPH VARGO AND JOSEPH IORILLO

PUBLISHED BY MONOLITH GRAPHICS
CLEVELAND, OHIO, USA
WWW.MONOLITHGRAPHICS.COM

---



Cover and Interior Artwork by Joseph Vargo
Design and Layout by Christine Filipak

Publisher's Cataloging-in-Publication Data
The Legend of Darklore Manor and Other Tales of Terror
by Joseph Vargo and Joseph Iorillo
ISBN: 0-9788857-6-7
ISBN(13): 978-0-9788857-6-2
1. fiction—horror, ghost stories
2. Vargo, Joseph 3. Iorillo, Joseph

Made in the USA

---

Catherine Elizabeth Belle 2010

# The Legend of Darklore Manor

## AND OTHER TALES OF TERROR

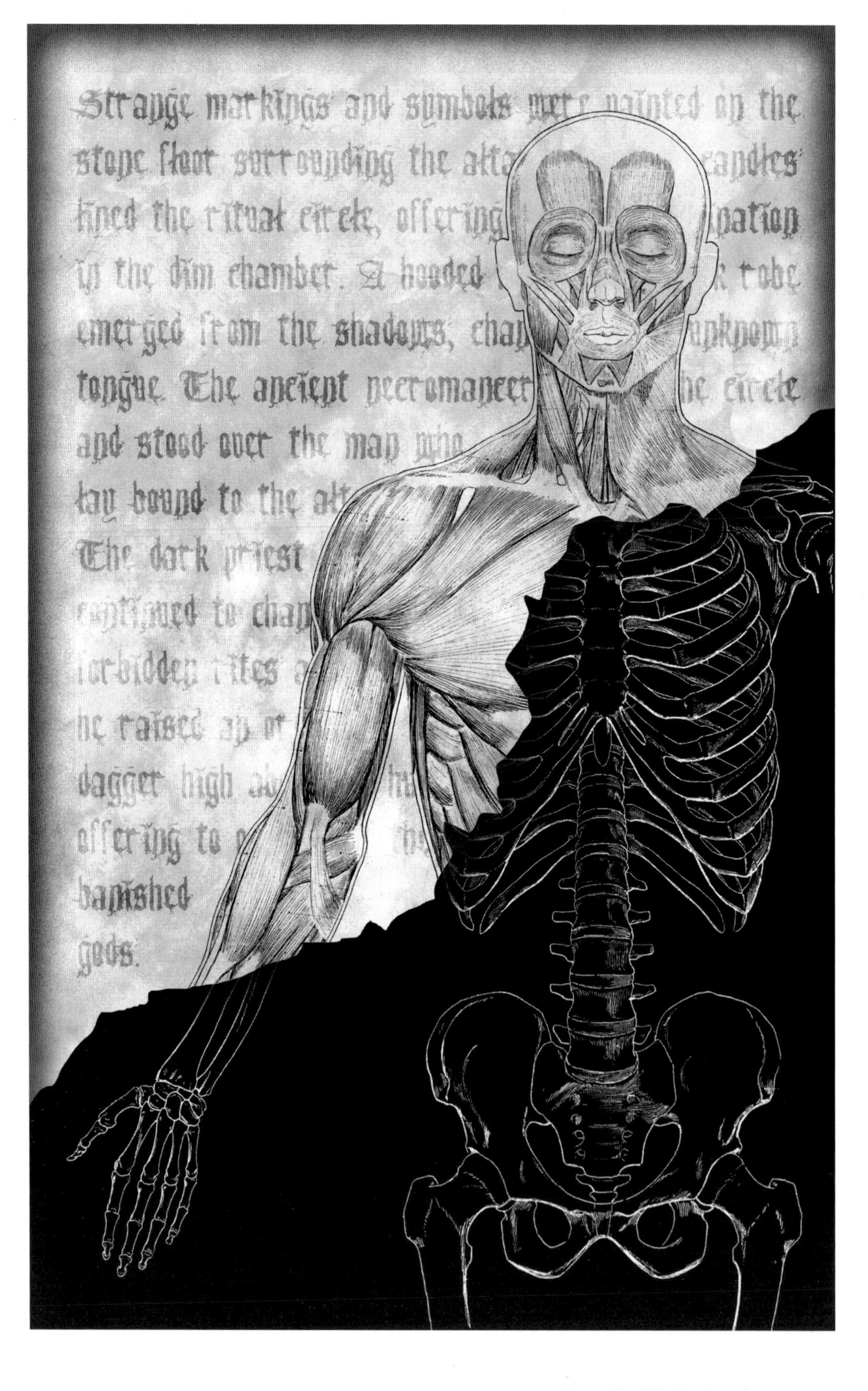

Strange markings and symbols were painted on the
stone floor surrounding the candles
lined the ritual circle, offering
in the dim chamber. A hooded robe
emerged from the shadows, unknown
tongue. The ancient necromancer the circle
and stood over the man who
lay bound to the
The dark priest
continued to
forbidden rites
he raised up
dagger high
offering to
banished
gods.

# THE CORONER

*by Joseph Vargo and Joseph Iorillo*

It was just after midnight when the doors to the city morgue swung open, interrupting Jack Caldwell's otherwise quiet night. A stocky paramedic pushed his gurney to the side of Jack's cold steel examination table, then pulled back the sheet to reveal the body of an elderly man dressed in a dark suit and conservative red-striped tie. The old man looked to be about seventy years of age, and even in death, the gray-haired gent looked distinguished.

Jack's eyes shifted back to the paramedic who was staring curiously at the cadaver.

"Found him at a bus stop on Grove Street," the paramedic explained. "Just sitting there on the bench, waiting to get picked up. All dressed up with no place to go."

Jack smirked at the paramedic's limp attempt at humor, then asked, "Any wallet or I.D.?"

"No, but you're gonna love this." The paramedic picked up an evidence bag from between the dead man's polished black shoes and handed it to the assistant medical examiner. "This was all he had in his pockets."

Jack took the bag and examined its contents through the clear plastic to discover a spool of thick thread and a large curved sewing needle. He glanced back at the paramedic and caught him staring at a steel tray beside the autopsy slab. There, amid the serrated bone saws and razor sharp scalpels that were used to severe limbs and filet human flesh, was a similar-looking needle and a spool of heavy surgical suture.

The paramedic raised his eyebrows. "Maybe I should've checked him for stitches."

This time Jack didn't respond. He knew what the paramedic was referring to, but it was considered bad taste to discuss the topic around the coroner's office. He gave the paramedic a cold stare as he grabbed the old man beneath the arms. The paramedic took hold of the dead man's feet and transferred him to the autopsy table. Jack scribbled his signature on the paramedic's clipboard and handed it back to him.

As he wheeled the empty gurney out of the room, the paramedic couldn't resist leaving Jack with a parting remark. "I'll just leave you two alone."

There was virtually no pressure to working the graveyard shift in the city morgue. After six months as assistant medical examiner, Jack did little more than undress and wash the bodies, log them in, and administer a preliminary examination, leaving the more unpleasant work for the day shift. As he began to prep his post-mortem guest, Jack thought back to the paramedic's comments about checking the old man's body for stitches. He was referring to an infamous unsolved homicide case in the city's history. It was a taboo subject, but now Jack couldn't get it out of his head. Six bodies had been found over the last twenty or so years. The victims had all shared the same gruesome, inexplicable fate. They had all been discovered dressed in suits, and in each case, the victim's heart was missing. The bodies were vivisected and neatly sewn back together. The papers and local media had dubbed the ritualistic killer 'The Coroner.'

Jack's curiosity was piqued. As he removed the dead man's jacket and tie and began to unbutton his shirt, Jack discovered an unusual metal pendant around the old man's neck. At first glance it appeared to be a strange and intricately carved medallion, but on closer inspection Jack realized that it was actually an ornate skeleton key. This odd token seemed somehow fitting, considering the old man's other personal effects. Jack set the key down on the examination table and resumed his work.

As he carefully unbuttoned the man's shirt, a mesmerizing tapestry of tattoo-work adorning the dead man's upper body revealed itself. The design was unlike anything Jack had ever seen and seemed completely out of place on a man of this age. It appeared to be some sort of tribal motif with black spidery arms flaring out from the center of the corpse's chest to entwine themselves around the man's torso and upper arms. The central pattern was a complex mass of scrollwork that formed a shape resembling an old lock. It seemed at once Celtic and Oriental, some baffling mystical emblem that conjured up thoughts of dark magic and unspeakable rituals. At the very heart of the design was a small dark slit that penetrated the man's flesh.

Jack picked up a thin surgical probe and inserted the tip of the instrument into the opening. The probe disappeared into the slit a full two inches before he removed it. Jack set the probe down beside the key that he had found around the old man's neck, unease and bewilderment growing inside of him. He glanced back at the lock-shaped design that surrounded the opening in the dead man's chest and a strange thought occurred to him. Jack picked up the key and paused for a moment to contemplate the macabre ramifications of what he was about to do, then he inserted the key into the dead man's sternum. It was a perfect fit.

Jack drew a deep breath, then turned the key.

The instant the key turned full circle, a burning cold pain, not unlike an electrical jolt, surged through Jack's body. He stood frozen in place, unable to move or relinquish his grip on the key. He watched in horror as the spidery arms of the tattoo slowly began to stir and writhe beneath the dead man's skin, as if awakening from a deep, ancient slumber. The serpentine tendrils strained against the man's withered flesh until they began to tear through it. Oily black tentacles wrapped themselves around Jack's hand and slowly began to slither and climb up his arm, and as they did, the burning cold pain was replaced by a numbing sensation.

This is not happening, Jack thought. Dear God, I'm imagining this. But his own panicked thoughts were replaced by a sudden onrush of brutal mental images that seemed to come from nowhere. He saw men with their eyes wide with shock, their trembling hands held up to ward off the furious, incomprehensible black storm rushing at them. The dark phantom that engulfed the men was possessed with a diabolic, ancient hunger and madness, beyond any human evil Jack had read or heard about. Jack saw the victims being devoured from inside as if from a fast-moving, corrosive cancer. His head throbbed with the monstrous hate emanating from the horrifying tattoo that had sprung to life. Whatever had caused this gargantuan hatred was lost in the mists of time, but the diabolic Thing still remembered and would never forget. Its hunger would never die. Jack wondered what hellish Pandora's Box he had opened. He could feel the mass of tentacles squirming and undulating beneath his shirt as the spidery arms sprawled across his chest. The sounds of human torment pierced Jack's ears. The echo of wails and lamentations accompanied the nightmarish visions that flooded his mind, revealing a chain of countless victims stretching back through time. Eventually the flurry of images came into focus, forcing Jack to bear witness to an arcane ceremony. He saw a black altar that held a human captive, a young, dazed man, bound to the ebony slab by thick ropes. Strange markings and symbols were painted on the stone floor surrounding the altar. Blood red candles lined the ritual circle, offering the only illumination in the dim chamber. A hooded figure in a black robe emerged from the shadows, chanting in an unknown tongue.

The ancient necromancer entered the circle and stood over the man who lay bound to the altar. The dark priest continued to chant forbidden rites as he raised an ornate dagger high above his human offering to one of the banished gods. The sorcerer plunged the blade deep into the center of the victim's chest, impregnating him with the raging vengeance that would go on and on forever. And then Jack Caldwell's last shreds of consciousness slipped away.

In the morning when Kelly Campbell, the day shift M.E., arrived to relieve Jack, she found the old man's body in peaceful repose, vivisected and neatly sewn closed. The toe tag read John Doe 004459. Even the death certificate had been meticulously filled out, listing the man's death as 'heart failure, due to natural causes.'

Kelly turned and was startled to see Jack standing closely behind her. "You've been a busy bee," she said, taking a step back.

Jack offered her a devious grin. "I was inspired." Then he picked up the skeleton key medallion from the instrument tray and slipped it around his neck.

"Key to your heart?" Kelly asked.

"Not exactly," Jack said with a wink. Then he tucked the key in his shirt and quickly buttoned the top few buttons, hoping she wouldn't notice the newly acquired knotwork of black tendrils that snaked across his chest.

# BLACK HEART

*by Joseph Vargo*

"So you want proof of the supernatural—monsters and witches and things that ain't supposed to be? Well then, Mr. Morgan, meet me at Black Bayou Junction, tonight at 10. Come alone... and don't be late."

The phone call from the mystery woman was cryptic, but it had piqued my curiosity enough to convince me to meet with her. I'd had my share of weird calls and letters since I began writing for Shadow Hunter magazine, but I was always pretty good at weeding out the kooks. Maybe it was a prank to send me on a wild goose chase, but her low, throaty voice sounded kind of sexy, and since I had no plans for the evening, I decided to take a drive. It was already after 9:00, so I grabbed my camera and ran.

After a harrowing ride through unlit country backroads, I arrived at the desolate crossroads a few minutes late. She was already there, smoking a cigarette as she sat behind the wheel of a late-model pickup. Her long black hair reflected the moonlight. I guessed her age to be about twenty-five. In the red glow from her cigarette, I could see that she was even more attractive than her voice had led me to believe. "You're late, Mr. Morgan," she said. "Get in." Her startlingly flat, commanding tone made me climb in without a word. "I'm Nicole," she said as she threw the truck in gear, "and I'll be your hostess for this evening." With that, she floored the gas pedal and we were off.

We drove for about twenty minutes along a narrow backroad, during which time she kept the conversation limited to small talk, skillfully avoiding the topic of where we were headed. Finally, she pulled over and parked along the road. She got out and said "This way," motioning with her head toward the woods. I followed a few steps behind her as we proceeded to make our way along an overgrown path. Thick vines entwined throughout the woods and moss hung heavy from the branches of dead trees. After a short trek through the black forest, we came upon a ramshackle mansion in the middle of the misty bayou. The place had become a haven for crows who had taken to roost upon every ledge and cornice of the dilapidated manor. The girl began walking to the house, but I grabbed her arm.

"Hold it. I'm not trespassing on private property until you tell me what's going on."

"All right," she whispered, then lit another cigarette, "but I doubt if you'll believe me." For the first time that night, her strong, commanding voice softened, becoming more solemn and reflective. "It was six years ago when my boyfriend Eric talked me into venturing into the swamp one night in search of a local legend. I didn't really want to go, but I figured it was the least I could do for the guy who had my name tattooed over his heart. When we were kids we had all heard stories about a place called Hangman's Hollow, where vigilante justice took its toll on those accused of practicing witchcraft and the black arts. The bodies of 13 witches were supposed to be buried beneath the old hanging tree in the middle of the swamp. A rotting rope dangled from one of the branches of the tree, supposedly the remnants of the hangman's noose, and stories told that if you swung from the rope at midnight, the dead would claw their way out of the ground and try to drag you down into their graves with them." She smiled and shook her head. "We never did come across that old hanging tree that night, but we sure as hell did find something."

The girl gazed off into the distance as if looking back into the past. "It didn't take us long to get lost in the bayou. We tried staying on dry ground, but soon we found ourselves surrounded by mist, and wading through an endless bog. The swamp bubbled and the mossy water rippled to reveal the presence of things slithering just beneath the surface. After a while, we heard a strange sound in the distance, rising above the serenade of crickets and frogs. It sounded like the growling of a large animal, followed by a low wailing cry.

"Against my better judgement, we followed the sounds through a dense area of vines and withered trees to a small clearing where an old shack stood. The moans were coming from a root cellar shed behind the decrepit hut. As we slowly approached the shed to investigate, we could hear feral growls, deep and guttural, between the moans. We got about twenty feet away from the shed when we were startled by a light from behind us and we ducked for cover in a nearby thicket. The door of the shack creaked open and a hunched figure came out, holding a lantern high.

"Who's there?" a gravelly voice croaked. We remained silent and still for what seemed like an eternity until the voice whispered once more, "Who's there?" The figure passed in front of us and I could see that it was an old woman who looked like she had aged beyond death itself. She hobbled to the shed and unlocked the storm cellar doors. I wanted to run, but Eric had an iron grip on my wrist and held me fast. The old hag threw open the thick wooden doors and we could hear the sloshing sound of heavy footsteps slowly climbing the root cellar stairs. A shambling form, cloaked in shadows, emerged from the black pit to tower over her. The thing stood a full foot taller than the old crone and swayed before her, growling lowly. She held forth a jar and began whispering strange words. As the incantation grew louder, the thing grew silent and still. She pointed a bony finger in the direction we were hiding and the thing turned and began to move toward us."

The girl shivered, then took a long drag from her cigarette. "We ran through the woods until we were both out of breath. We were fast, but the creature was unrelenting and we could hear it following our trail, getting closer with every step. Eric and I were both exhausted as we ran through a large clearing, but we made it to the other side and tried to hide behind some trees at the hollow's edge. We heard the growling sound grow louder, announcing the creature's approach. After a few seconds, the thing emerged from the shadows and we could see it more clearly in the moonlight. The thing looked like a scarecrow slowly shambling across the hollow. It stood well over six feet tall, and it was clad in tattered remnants of a long black coat. The creature lurched and swayed as if it were a life-sized marionette being controlled by some unseen puppeteer.

"We were quiet and still as the thing ambled past us, but then it suddenly stopped and turned its head in our direction. I could feel my heart pounding as the creature stood before us. It raised its head as if to detect our scent in the wind then began to step toward us. Eric leapt out at the thing with his cigarette lighter, hoping to startle it with the flame. I could tell Eric was scared, but he wanted to defend me. And the pitiful, small flame did briefly fend-off the creature. The flame touched the thing's tattered cloak and it began to smolder, then burn. Soon the creature was engulfed in flames and blindly stumbled into the swamp. I was terrified. I began running, and I ran all through the night."

"What happened to him, your boyfriend?"

"I never spoke to him again after that night."

"That's a wild story," I said, trying not to sound too unsympathetic, "but it doesn't prove a thing. And what the hell has it got to do with this God-forsaken place?"

"You want proof, Mr. Morgan? Proof of witches and monsters and things that go bump in the night? Well, it's waiting for you inside that old house." Just then, a blood-curdling moan from inside the mansion broke the still of the night. "Come on," she said.

We entered the immense house through a broken door under the watchful eyes of the sentinel crows. The girl's flashlight revealed dust-covered furniture, tapestries and paintings, all of them hinting sadly at the former elegance of the old plantation. We made our way to the entrance hall and headed upstairs. Ever so cautiously, we ascended the creaking staircase. The second floor had a gaping hole in the roof that allowed the crows to access the attic interior, and shadows fluttered overhead on black wings.

"Did you know that certain cultures believe that crows and ravens carry the souls of the dead into the netherworld?" the girl asked me. She opened her hand to reveal several voodoo wards. One of them looked like a crow's severed foot clutching a dark red stone in its talons. She held the crow's claw before her as if it were a lantern to guide her in the dark and followed its unseen light into a room at the end of the hall. She opened an antique cabinet to reveal six large jars that each held what looked like a human heart suspended in a dark liquid. She held the talisman out and moved it in front of the jars until her hand began to shake before a jar holding a heart as black as coal. Her eyes welled with tears and she picked up the jar.

Rats scurried across the rotting floorboards as we returned to the dilapidated entry hall of the manor. She walked along with the jar held out in front of her as if the black heart within were now guiding her. My own heart pounding with dread, I followed her as she made her way into an old library. Cobwebs and dust were all that remained on the empty bookshelves that lined the walls of the room. She stopped in the center of the room and pulled back a decayed area rug to reveal a trap door that led down into the cellar. We made our way down the creaking steps.

The bones of possums and rats littered the floor. I could hear the sound of heavy chains grinding against stone, and then a hulking shape rose up from the shadows. My eyes widened, trying to see better in the dark, and my throat constricted with terror. The thing lunged forward into the meager light, but stopped short of reaching us, restrained by a collar and thick shackles that secured it to the wall. The creature clawed and snapped at us, growling and frothing at the mouth. Its skin was grayish-yellow and drawn tight over his skeletal frame. His eyes were glazed over with cataracts and sunken deep into the sockets of his cadaverous face. His lips were drawn back in a deathly grimace and the top of his skull was missing, as if it had been blown off by a violent blast to the head. The creature emitted a sickening stench of rot and decay, and even though half of his head was gone and his rotting brains were exposed, the thing was alive and standing there before us.

"I've been searching for years," the girl said. "You're the first person I've told the entire story to. Well, not the entire story, I haven't finished it yet. You see, after Eric set that creature on fire, I heard a loud blast, then I saw Eric fall to the ground. The old hag was standing over his body with a shotgun, smoke rising from the barrel. That was the last I saw of him. I ran and never looked back. Eventually I made it out of the swamp, but Eric never returned. I never told the police the entire story, only the part about the old woman and her shack. They searched the area and found the house, but it was deserted. They never found any traces of the hag or her walking corpse. After months of searching on my own, I tracked them down to this God-forsaken place." She shone her flashlight onto the creature's chest. A jagged scar was sealed closed by crude stitches, right beneath a tattoo that read "Nicole."

"Oh my God," I whispered.

The girl's eyes glittered. "It was easy to kill the old woman while she slept. Then I found the jar with the zombie's heart, and I smashed it. The creature seemed to cave in on itself, as if it were made of rotting paper. I knew the corpses of the hag's victims would be buried near the house, and it wasn't long before I unearthed Eric's remains. He was the love of my life. You have to understand that. I couldn't bear to live without him, no matter what."

I tried to speak but I could not. My heart raced, making me dizzy and breathless.

The abomination in chains mewled and hissed. The girl's pale hand clutched my arm with surprising strength, inching me closer to the creature. "I'm so sorry, Mr. Morgan, but Eric gets so hungry... and after all, you wanted proof."

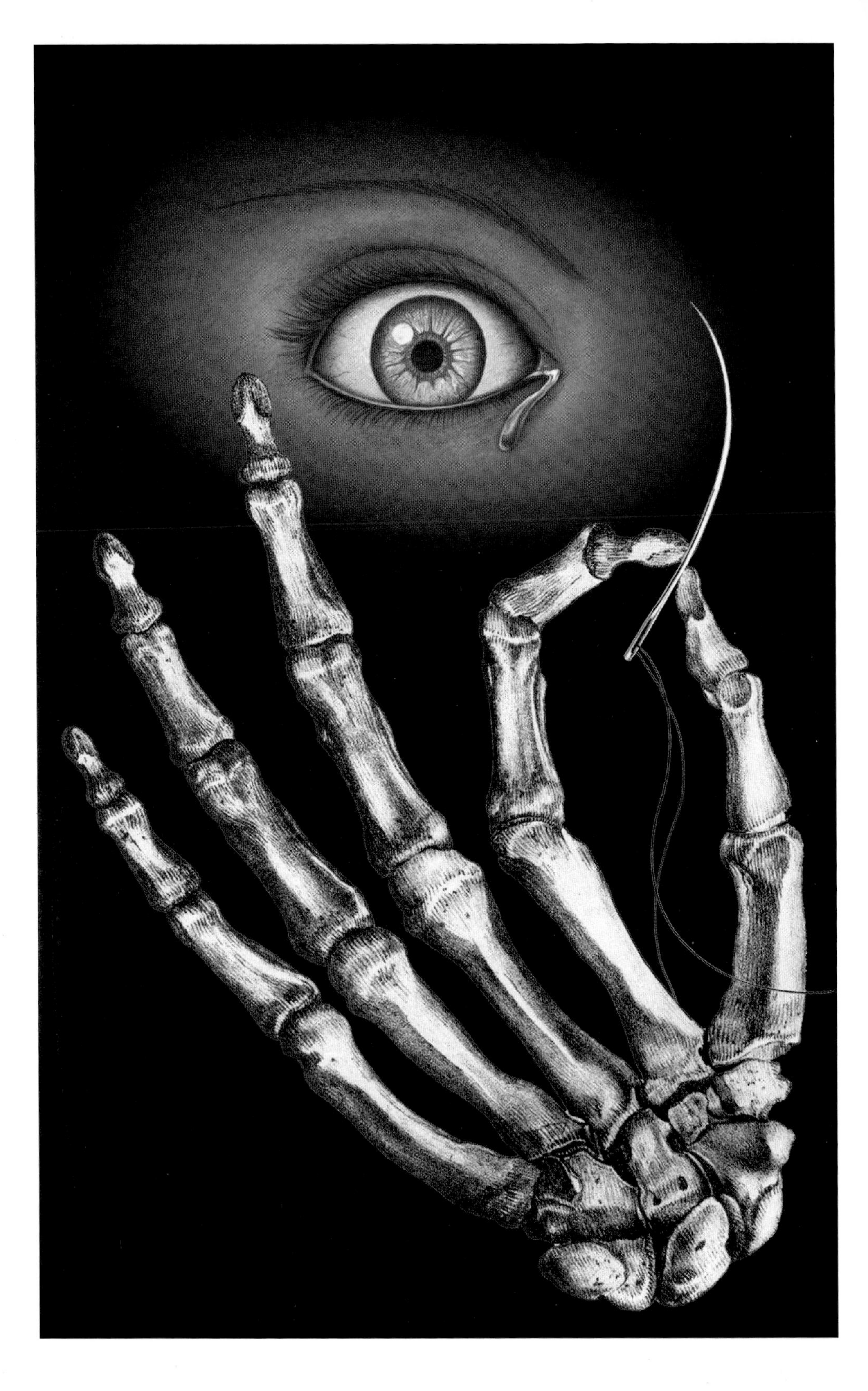

# MR. STITCH

*by Joseph Iorillo and Joseph Vargo*

Detective Vaughn pulled up in front of the large white Colonial home on Ford Avenue a few seconds after the ambulance had sped away to Crawford Memorial Hospital. The piercing wail of the siren could still be heard in the distance. It was just after 3 a.m. and several neighbors stood on their porches in bathrobes and pajamas, staring at the proceedings.

Vaughn got out of his car and motioned to Sergeant McCafferty, who stood with two other uniformed officers on the perfectly manicured lawn. "How bad is it?" Vaughn asked.

"Bad," McCafferty said, "I've never seen anything like it."

"What do we have?"

"Two victims, both female, both fifteen years old, assaulted by some unknown intruder."

The detective clenched his jaw, then asked "What happened to them?"

McCafferty consulted a small, hand-held notebook then said "The first girl, Beth Davis, had her mouth sewn shut. The second one, the Stefano girl, had her eyes sewn shut."

"Angela Stefano?"

"Yeah," McCafferty whispered.

Vaughn's heart sank. Everyone in their small town knew Angela Stefano had been dealt more than her share of tragedy. Her father and mother had died in a car crash when she was eight, leaving her in the custody of an uncle with a drug problem. Last year, that uncle died of a morphine overdose, leaving her an orphan for the second time. The uncle's second wife was now her guardian.

It was a warm spring night, but Vaughn felt a deep chill. He glanced at the house. "Whose house is it?"

"Another girl lives here, Carrie Childress. Her parents are out of town for the weekend. She's still inside with two of her other friends. They were all having a slumber party."

"Any alcohol?"

McCafferty nodded. "Two empty bottles of wine. You can smell it on them."

Vaughn sighed and headed for the front door, but the old sergeant touched his elbow. "They were drinking, but I don't think any of them could have been responsible for something like this," McCafferty said. "They're really shaken up."

Inside, the three remaining teenage girls huddled on the couch in the living room with a female uniformed officer standing behind them.

"Which one of you is Carrie Childress?" Vaughn asked softly.

A small red-haired girl looked up at him fearfully, then looked away again.

Vaughn focused on the girl. "Carrie? Do you want to tell me what happened?"

"I already told her," Carrie murmured, glancing at the female officer.

"I want you to tell me," Vaughn said.

"I woke up about an hour ago," Carrie said, looking at her two friends. "I had to go to the bathroom. We were all in my room. The night-light was on, and I saw… I saw them in their sleeping bags. Angela was gasping and crying, and Beth was unconscious. She was covered in blood. Her mouth…." Carrie began to tremble. One of her friends put her arm around Carrie's twitching shoulders. "That's all I remember."

"Who did this to them?"

"I don't know," Carrie said,

Vaughn looked at the hands and clothing of the girls. No blood was evident. "You didn't see anyone else in the house but you girls?"

"I didn't see anyone," Carrie said softly, "and all the doors were locked." The other two girls said the same thing when Vaughn posed the question to them.

The detective sighed and took the female officer aside. "You questioned them separately?" Vaughn asked.

"Yes. For what it's worth, their stories are the same."

Snapping on a pair of latex gloves so he wouldn't contaminate the crime scene, Vaughn climbed the stairs with the female police officer and looked around Carrie's bedroom. He crouched and looked over the sleeping bags, studying the spatter of blood on two of the bags.

"That's Beth's sleeping bag," the officer said, pointing at the bag with the heaviest blood stains. Vaughn, however, was studying Angela's bag. Hidden within the folds of the fabric, he discovered a length of thick black sewing thread attached to a long curved needle that was stained with blood. He placed the needle and thread into a clear evidence bag and sealed it shut, then slid it into his overcoat pocket.

Next to Angela's sleeping bag, several droplets of blood seemed to trail off toward the door. He followed the trail across the carpet and down the hallway to a door that he found locked. At the end of the hall, an ornate wall mirror reflected back his tired, grim face, an expression of perplexity lining his features. "Whose room is this?" Vaughn asked the female cop, but to his surprise, Carrie answered, standing at the top of the stairs.

"My brother, Davey. He's away at college. He likes to keep his room locked when he's gone."

Davey Childress. The name was vaguely familiar to Vaughn. The kid had had his share of run-ins with the cops over the years. Underage drinking, fighting, even threatening the life of a former girlfriend.

Vaughn deftly popped open the door's flimsy lock using a flat, credit card-sized slip of metal he kept in his wallet for just such occasions, but there was nothing of interest in Davey's room. The bed had been stripped of its sheets, and the closet had been emptied of clothes. A subtle layer of dust lay over everything.

Out on the porch, Vaughn told Sergeant McCafferty to phone the hospital and tell the doctors that he would need to talk to Angela and Beth tonight, as soon as possible.

The Beth Davis who lay in a semi-private room in the pediatric wing of Crawford Memorial bore little resemblance to the pretty, vivacious Beth Davis pictured in the high school yearbook that had been sitting in the Childress living room. After sending Beth's distraught parents out of the room, Vaughn pulled up a chair to her bedside, trying not to betray the shock he felt at seeing the ruined lower half of her face. The heavy black thread that her demented assailant had used to stitch up her mouth had been removed and the ragged holes had been more carefully repaired with fine white sutures. Her lips were swollen and droplets of blood still oozed from her wounds onto the swath of gauze wound around her face.

"How do you feel?"

"Sleepy," she whispered, trying her best not to move her mouth. "Numb."

"I know it probably hurts to talk, but I need you to tell me who did this to you. Was it one of the other girls?"

"No. I was passed out. Don't remember much. Woke up… and I was like this." Fresh tears spilled from her eyes.

"How much did you have to drink, Beth?"

She shrugged. "Three glasses. Maybe four."

Vaughn sat back in his chair. She was a slight girl. That was more than enough alcohol to knock her out for a while. "What were you girls doing just before you went to bed?"

"Telling ghost stories. Trying to scare each other. We talked about boys. About who we liked."

"Which boys in particular did you talk about?"

Beth looked alarmed. She shut her eyes, shaking her head. "I don't want to talk anymore. Please."

Vaughn patted her hand. "It's all right. Get some sleep."

Angela Stefano sat in a chair by the window as dawn bled into the turbulent indigo sky. Although she seemed to be studying the horizon, heavy bandages were wrapped around her eyes.

"You should be in bed," Vaughn said.

"Are you with the police?"

"I'm Detective Mike Vaughn. Your aunt is getting some coffee. She said I could speak with you about what happened."

"Did you ask Beth?"

"Yes," Vaughn said, sitting on the edge of her bed. "But I'd like to hear it from you."

"I don't remember much." Angela's voice sounded flat, drugged.

"That implies you remember something. What is it?"

Angela turned her head in his direction, and Vaughn nearly winced at the sight of the blood smears on the bandages in the vicinity of her eyes. "Do you know the legend of Mr. Stitch?" Her voice quivered as she mentioned the name.

"No. Who is that?"

"Long ago, when two people wanted to make sure that a secret or a promise would be kept, they made a pact over a sewing needle and thread. Once they shared their secret, or swore their promise, they would recite this poem...

*This secret promise, I swear to keep,*
*Shared in trust, then buried deep —*
*Cross my heart and hope to die,*
*Stick a needle in my eye —*
*If I should tell a living soul,*
*May Mr. Stitch come take his toll —*
*And while I lie asleep in bed,*
*Seal my lips with sewing thread.*"

Vaughn said nothing. The poem's chilling lines and Angela's singsong lilt made him uneasy.

"After reciting the poem," Angela said, "the two would bury the needle and thread in a graveyard. If either of the people broke their vow or told the secret, Mr. Stitch would pay them a visit at night. With needle and thread in hand, he would creep into their bedrooms to sew their mouths closed while they slept. If his victims awoke, Mr. Stitch would sew their eyes shut to keep them from seeing him."

"Did you and the other girls recite the poem earlier tonight?"

Angela nodded.

"Beth said you had been talking about boys. About the boys you liked. I'm guessing you each swore an oath of secrecy. Did Beth break her promise?"

Angela said nothing.

"Did you break the oath, too?"

"No," Angela said after a moment. "But I saw him. That's why he hurt me."

Vaughn leaned forward. "Who did you see, Angela? What did he look like?"

She swallowed, trying to maintain her composure and her wounded eyes strained to fight back painful tears. "I saw his face. I'll never be able to forget it—those cruel eyes squinting at me, that evil smile and the thick black strands of thread dangling from the curved needle in his hand."

"Who?" Vaughn asked, "Who did you see?"

Angela's lips trembled as she whispered "It was Mr. Stitch."

Vaughn's brow furled. "The man from your story?"

"Yes," she said quietly.

Unable to make sense of her response, he tried to redirect his line of questioning. "How did he get inside the house?"

"He came out of our nightmares," Angela's voice quivered. "He crept beside her and climbed on top of her. I couldn't do anything. I couldn't stop him."

As gently but as persistently as he dared, he peppered her with further questions—how tall was this assailant, how old, what color hair, what type of clothing. But Angela kept shaking her head, finally turning back to the window. The sound of soft sniffling indicated that she was weeping.

The next day, Vaughn sat at his desk in the squadroom, files and notes spread out before him like pieces of a jigsaw puzzle. In fact, they seemed to be pieces of separate jigsaw puzzles. He tried to organize the fragments into a coherent picture of the mysterious and sinister Mr. Stitch.

Sergeant McCafferty dropped a sheaf of papers on top of Vaughn's already cluttered blotter. "From the doctors. The results of blood tests on the two girls. No hallucinogenic drugs in their systems, just alcohol. You making any progress?"

"Not much. I thought Davey Childress was a solid lead but I called the university and got a handful of people who can alibi him for that night." The detective hesitated then asked "Have you ever heard an urban legend about a character named Mr. Stitch?"

McCafferty looked at him with a puzzled expression. "What's he supposed to be, like the bogey man or something?"

"Yeah. Something like that. Have you ever heard the name before?"

"No. Why?"

"Just a story one of the girl's mentioned. I haven't pieced it all together yet, but something really shook them up."

"So what do you think happened in that house last night, Mike?"

Vaughn sat back in his swivel chair. "Tipsy girls telling scary stories, revealing secret crushes. I checked the cell phone records of the girls. Around one a.m., Beth called a boy named Kevin Leonetti and told him that Carrie Childress liked him. Kevin told me it was a short phone call, and he could hear a couple other girls giggling in the background before she hung up."

"Sounds like the secret crushes weren't that secret."

Vaughn's thoughts returned to the enigmatic Mr. Stitch and his grisly duty to ensure that secrets were kept, whatever the cost.

Beth Davis seemed to be in better shape the following day when Inspector Vaughn visited her at home. They sat outside on the patio, and Beth had a difficult time meeting the detective's eyes. She kept fidgeting with the small crucifix hanging around her neck.

"I told you I don't remember much about that night. I was drunk."

"You don't remember calling Kevin Leonetti while Carrie was out of the room and telling him that Carrie had a crush on him?"

Beth shook her head. "What difference does it make, anyway?"

Vaughn shrugged. "You broke your promise." He did not have to add the unspoken consequence of breaking her promise: the wrath of Mr. Stitch. He could see the fear in Beth's eyes. Her fingers clutched at the crucifix and she appeared even more annoyed and agitated than before.

"I don't want to talk about this anymore!" she cried. "Why don't you leave me alone?"

"Don't you want me to catch whoever did this to you?"

"You can't," she said suddenly. Her eyes welled with tears.

"Beth, Mr. Stitch isn't real."

She stood up and was about to run back in the house, but Vaughn touched her on the arm. "Beth, please. Let's talk about what happened that night —"

"No! You're not going to make me break my promise! It's been more than a year and I'm still not going to tell!" She stormed back inside the house, nearly running into her mother, Denise, who was standing by the patio door.

Vaughn's brow furrowed. What was she talking about? Beth had already broken her promise regarding Carrie's affection for Kevin. It's been a year.... What other secret was she referring to?

Denise stepped out onto the patio, clutching her sweater

around her as a cool breeze stirred the leaves on the trees. "I'm sorry," she said. "She's still traumatized."

"It's understandable."

"She's had a lot to deal with lately. She's struggling in school, her brother's been dealing with diabetes, her father's lawn care business isn't doing so well… now this." Denise glanced worriedly back into the house. She cleared her throat. She looked strained and tired. "Detective, do you think a person is responsible for what happened? I mean, what kind of person could do something like this to another human being?"

"A very sick person," he answered solemnly.

"Beth is afraid to go to sleep. She's afraid that her nightmares will come to life."

"Mrs. Davis, Mr. Stitch is just a story. He's not real."

"Well, my daughter's injuries are very real." She tried to keep the anger from her voice. She shook her head. "You know, as bad as I feel for what happened to Beth, I feel even worse for poor Angela. She's had a terrible year. First that terrible uncle of hers dies, now this."

"Did you know her uncle?" Vaughn asked.

"I knew that I didn't care for him."

"Why?"

"It wasn't just the drugs. He just seemed… evil. He would get a little too friendly with Beth when she went over there. It made her uncomfortable. And sometimes he would look at Angela like…." She lowered her eyes as if embarrassed. "I don't know if he ever touched her. But he seemed like the type."

Vaughn said nothing.

Denise looked off at the swaying trees as the sun slipped behind a cloud. "I know it sounds silly, I know he's dead, but I get the feeling that he's responsible for this."

The following evening, as Vaughn sat and blankly stared at the mess of files on his desk, the medical reports, the stacks of crime scene photos, and the coroner's report on Angela's uncle, he came to agree with Mrs. Davis.

Angela was still in the hospital, but the bandages had been removed from her eyes. Her scarred and torn eyelids looked pitiful, and her eyes were bloodshot, with angry scratches on her corneas and irises. She sat by the window contemplating the night.

"Angela," Vaughn said. "How are you feeling?"

"Okay. They'll let me go home tomorrow." She tried to smile. "It's hard for me to see, but I'm getting bored just lying in bed. I don't want to fall asleep. I don't want the nightmares to return."

Vaughn sat on the edge of her bed. He said nothing for a while. "Beth isn't very good at keeping secrets, is she?" he finally said. "The secret about Carrie and Kevin, for instance. That probably had you worried. Worried that her tongue would get even looser and she'd start to reveal other secrets."

"What are you talking about?"

"Your uncle. His death. It was ruled an accidental overdose, but even the coroner wondered in his notes why there were traces of insulin in the needle. The insulin sent him into shock, then into cardiac arrest. Your uncle had such a colorful drug history that the strange mixture was written off as just another example of his reckless experimentation. But we know what it really was, don't we?"

Angela stared at him. Her expression was unreadable.

"How long had he been molesting you, Angela?"

"I don't want to talk about my uncle."

"Beth's younger brother has diabetes. You got her to steal some of his insulin. You mixed it with your uncle's morphine. And when he died, you swore her to secrecy."

"I don't know what you're talking about."

Vaughn removed the police evidence bag from his overcoat pocket and set it down on the bed beside him. Angela's injured eyes welled with tears when she saw the sewing needle and thread inside.

"Angela," Vaughn said, "we have to talk about what really happened that night."

"I told you what happened. It was Mr. Stitch."

"No it wasn't," Vaughn said softly, "He's not real. He's just a story that you made up to keep Beth quiet. He doesn't exist."

"Yes he does," Angela insisted, "I saw him!"

"Where did you see him?"

"In Carrie's house. He was standing at the end of the hall."

Vaughn's mind recollected the layout of Carrie's house, mentally following the trail of blood droplets down the corridor to where they ended in front of the locked room, and a grim realization swept over him.

"He was in the mirror," she whispered. "His evil eyes were glaring at me in the darkness. He was still holding the needle and thread in his bloody hand. You have to believe me."

Suddenly, the final piece of the puzzle fell into place. Vaughn stood up. "Angela, we'll get help for you. I promise."

The girl's lips curved into a slow, cold smile and her bloodshot eyes narrowed to a sinister squint. "There's no one to help her," she said in a raspy, masculine voice. "She must pay the price. She saw what no one must see. And she had to be punished. Just like the other one. They swore the pact, and she broke her promise. I had to pay her a visit."

Vaughn rushed from the room and ran down the hall. He had to find a nurse to get Angela sedated, and he had to get her admitted to the psychiatric ward as soon as possible before she hurt someone else. He found a young nurse in a room down the hall and practically wrenched her shoulder out of the socket dragging her back to Angela's room. When they entered the room, the nurse began screaming and Vaughn was left speechless by the grisly sight that greeted them.

Angela was staring at them both, blood raining from her ruined lips. Her scarred eyes reflected a distant expression of blissful madness. She was humming, and Vaughn imagined she was humming the ominous oath to Mr. Stitch. The needle and thread she had used to bind her mouth shut dangled from her crimson lips and the monstrous Mr. Stitch, his ghastly work complete, had retreated back into the shadows of her mind.

# DARKNESS IMMORTAL

*by Joseph Vargo*

My heart pounded in perfect time with the distant tolling of the old church bell as it struck the midnight hour. Concealed in shadow, I stood silently by the roadside as I watched the two moonlit silhouettes scale the tall iron rails of the old cemetery fence. The dark forms disappeared into the graveyard mists once they crossed the threshold of the dead.

Good sense alone should have held me there, or forced me to turn back and head for home, but instead, I drew a deep breath of the cool autumn air and proceeded to follow them. I slid the black satchel that I was carrying through the wrought iron bars of the fence, then paused once more to wonder how I had let myself get talked into this mess before I scaled the cemetery gate to trespass upon hallowed ground.

Once within the confines of the perimeter gate, I heard a rustling of dead leaves coming from beneath an ancient willow tree. They were there, in the shadows, waiting for me.

My eyes not yet accustomed to the darkness, I stepped cautiously toward the twisted willow. Suddenly, from across the cemetery, a beam of light swept over the field of gravestones, breaking the pitch blackness of the night. Before the light could reach me, a hand grabbed me from behind, pulling me into the shadows.

"It's just the old watchman," a voice behind me whispered,

breathless with apparent anxiety. It was J.D., and no matter how tough he tried to sound, his nervousness always betrayed him. The light slowly faded until at last it vanished completely into the misty dead of night. "He won't be back this way for a while."

I turned to face my two confederates who were well cloaked in the shadows. Even in the darkness, the two were easy to distinguish by the shape of their silhouettes. J.D. was the taller of the two. He looked like a lanky scarecrow and carried a half-empty bottle of Jack Daniels. The other one was built like a brick wall and carried a large sledge hammer slung over one broad shoulder. His name was Vic, and though he hadn't spoken a word, it was clear who was in charge. Ever since I'd known them, J.D. followed Vic's every command like a faithful dog.

Vic stepped out of the shadows and climbed up onto a headstone to survey the grounds. After quickly assessing that the coast was clear, he whispered "Let's go."

As silently as possible, we made our way through a crooked field of century-old, moss-covered tombstones. Once we had crossed the field of ancient graves, we came upon a monument chiseled in the likeness of an angel holding a sword. Vic stopped before the statue and set his sledge hammer down at the monument's base, then whispered "Give me the bag."

I handed him the leather satchel I was carrying and he opened it to retrieve a flashlight and a small, age-worn journal. The yellowed pages were tattered and covered with scratchy writing, arcane symbols and strange sketches. Vic studied the book beneath the flashlight's glow, then shifted the beam onto the angel's face. Following the direction of the statue's stern gaze, he guided the light toward a thick patch of woods at the farthest end of the cemetery. Vic handed the flashlight to J.D. and picked up the sledge hammer again, then said, "This way," and headed off toward the thicket.

We made our way through several yards of thorny bramble to discover a rusted gate, overgrown with vines. Tall crooked spikes protruded from the top of the gate, making the ancient barrier impossible to scale. J.D. pulled the vines from the gate and used the flashlight's beam to reveal an old lock. "We need a key," he whispered.

Vic stepped forward and said "Stand back," then, raising the sledge hammer from his shoulder, added "I got your key right here." Before anyone could utter a word in protest, Vic gave the lock two solid whacks, and with the groan of rusted iron, the ancient gate swung open.

Hesitantly, we ventured beyond the spiked perimeter fence and entered into a small clearing, dense with fog, where the rustle and flutter of crypt bats could be heard above the ghostly, whispering wind. After a few cautious steps, we saw something that made all three of us halt dead in our tracks.

Through the thick shroud of mist, a tall shadow loomed motionless at the center of the clearing. We slowly stepped toward the dark shape to to discover a grim monument—a tall tomb marker, crowned with the graven image of a human skull chiseled from black stone.

"Well, I'll be damned," Vic said.

J.D. directed his flashlight onto the monument where dead vines had entangled themselves around the base, half-covering an epitaph chiseled into the stone. He brushed the vines aside then struggled to read the inscription aloud, "Disturb ye not what lies buried here, lest ye wake what cannot die."

"What the hell is this place?" J.D. asked.

Vic answered "According to the journal, this is the tomb of Sebastian Drake."

"No way," J.D. said, lowering his voice to a breathy whisper as if afraid of disturbing the dead. "He's not real. That's just a story, like the freakin' bogeyman."

"Afraid not," Vic said, then paused to take a long swig from the bottle of Jack Daniels. "He's real... and he's buried right here." Vic set the sledge hammer down with a hard thud on the black sepulcher lid. The heavy stone slab was engraved with a large cross, surrounded by strange glyphs and wards.

"Who the hell is Sebastian Drake?" I asked.

"Oh yeah," Vic replied with a twisted grin, "that's right, you didn't grow up around here. You never heard the tales. He's a murderer, or at least he was, about a hundred and twenty years ago. Now he's just worm food."

J.D. offered a nervous laugh.

Vic handed the bottle to J.D., then continued "According to the legend, he was a sorcerer who practiced the black arts. The journal says Drake used a book called the Grimoire Mortis, which contained spells from the dreaded Ebon scrolls. He formed a coven that swore allegiance to the Dark Gods."

"They worshiped the Devil?" I asked.

"No. Not the Devil. Something much nastier," Vic said in a mockingly wicked tone. He picked up the journal and flipped through the age worn pages, then began to read aloud. "The Dark Gods were ancient beings that lived deep in the earth. They were terrible to behold and their desires were ravenous. They preyed upon mortal men and had an unquenchable thirst for human blood. As time passed, mankind grew to fear and shun them, and sought refuge from them. And the Dark Gods, their savage hungers denied, returned to the cavernous depths from which they came, to slumber and dwell in the shadows as darkness immortal." Vic snapped the journal shut and tossed it back into the satchel.

"Where'd you get that book?" J.D. asked.

Vic gave him a wink and said "Never you mind," then turned to me and continued. "Drake's coven held forbidden rituals and sacrifices on the two nights of the year when dark things supposedly arose to prowl the earth—Walpurgis night and Hallow's Eve."

The two of us stood there, staring speechlessly at Vic, as a grim realization began to sink in. He gave us a devious smile and said "Tell me this ain't the perfect place to spend Halloween."

"So why the hell is he buried here?" I asked.

"As the story goes, after some of the local kids started disappearing, the townspeople tracked Drake's little group down. The members of his coven were stoned to death, but Drake wasn't so lucky. They nailed him to a post and burned him alive. Then, just to be on the safe side, they cut off his head and buried his remains in hallowed ground. Their secret remained hidden for all these years, for over a century... until tonight." Vic approached the monument and locked his gaze on the black skull, perfectly sculpted to the most minute detail. "And now that we found his grave, I ain't leavin' without a souvenir." He took a step back, lifting the heavy hammer and said, "Shine your light on that skull."

J.D. stood frozen, and asked, "What are you gonna do?"

Vic gave him an icy stare for daring to question his order, and J.D. conceded to shine his flashlight beam onto the ebony death's head. Vic wrenched his hands tightly around the handle of the heavy hammer, raising it like a baseball bat, then swung the sledge with all his might. The hammer crashed against the monument at the base of the skull with a resounding crackle that echoed like thunder, sending shattered pieces of the black stone flying. Another violent hit sent a crack straight through the top of the ebony marker and a third strike sent the sinister chiseled skull toppling free from its tombstone base.

Vic burst into laughter as the skull hit the ground with a thud. The detached death's head rolled across the grave, and came to rest at my feet. I picked it up to examine its macabre detail in the moonlight.

Vic picked up the satchel and held it open before me, then smiled and said "Trick or treat."

I dropped the skull into the bag, happy to be rid of the accursed thing. Vic closed the satchel and set it on the ground, then picked up the sledge hammer again. He turned back toward the tomb and whispered, "Trick or treat you rotting, black-hearted corpse," then he slammed the hammer into the base of the monument.

"Wake up, Drake," he shouted. "It's Halloween! Wake up!" He continued his assault, furiously pounding on the lid, on the cross, on the obscure markings and sigils that covered the granite slab. Again and again he brought the sledge hammer down on the stone slab beneath his feet until a crack split the sepulcher lid in two.

The wind howled through the crack, sounding like the hiss and wail of some demonic beast. J.D. dropped the flashlight and bolted, and I followed close behind. As we ran through the woods, I could hear Vic laughing and shouting insults, followed by a thunderous sound and a mortal scream cut short.

J.D. stumbled out of the thicket and ran right into the outstretched arms of the night watchman.

"Hold it, right there," the old man ordered. The guard's hand was shaking as he withdrew his service revolver from its holster and directed his flashlight to scan the woods beyond. As soon as his light illuminated the broken gate, he uttered "Good Lord, what have you done?"

He marched us back through the gateway to see the extent of the damage we had inflicted. We reluctantly returned to the forsaken hollow to discover several heavy pieces of the shattered tomb lid lying overturned beside the unearthed grave. The watchman blessed himself with the sign of the cross then slowly crept toward the edge of the yawning tomb. He shone his flashlight into the open grave to find that it was empty, revealing only a gaping abyss of shadows and swirling mist.

J.D. picked up his flashlight from where he had dropped it, and turned its beam on the monument. The black skull had been replaced atop the marker. I stepped back from the tomb and nearly tripped over Vic who was sitting on the ground behind the gravestone. He was resting against the black monument, leaning back into the shadows, holding the satchel in his lap.

To this day, I don't know what twisted sense of curiosity compelled me to do what I did next, but I opened the satchel, and as I did, the watchman grabbed Vic by the shoulder and drew him into the light. Vic's face was frozen in a grisly leer, but to our awe and horror, it wasn't from atop his shoulders. His head was severed at the neck, as if torn from his body, and stared out at us from inside the black bag.

# GOLEM

*by Timothy Bennett and Joseph Vargo*

This is what death feels like. An icy grip seizing my very breath, damming the blood in my head and petrifying my body as I struggle to hold on to life. And the darkness before my eyes, so terrifying and bleak, coldly reflects the image of my death back at me.

All this I came to comprehend in my final fleeting moments, and with a grim certainty I realized that my demise was inescapable. Does my entire life now pass before me? No. I only see the events that have brought the Angel of Death to my company.

My 40th, and final, birthday came and went as most have, quietly... until late that evening. A pounding at the side door interrupted my solitude as a delivery person arrived with the unexpected, a crate big enough to hold gifts for all my birthdays combined. A second delivery person was hidden behind the monstrosity. I joined them in bringing the box to rest in the middle of my studio, leaving the crate standing like a wooden obelisk.

I almost didn't want to open it, wanting instead to relish in my excitement trying to determine what could be inside. As I signed for the crate, I was handed an accompanying envelope postmarked from Jerusalem. The handwriting was familiar, and when opened, the salutation was unmistakable.

A Gift from the Magi: Happy Birthday Bones. I bartered for this in my usual fashion. Some locals found this in a newly excavated crypt. Four magnificent guardian angels surrounded it on the floor above. You're not that good a friend to pay what they wanted for those, so got this thing from the basement. See you soon. — The Bobcat.

Bob was my best friend from college, and we kept in touch despite our different paths. He traveled the world searching for the meaning of life, while I remained safe at home letting life go by. Bones. That always made me laugh. Bob always said archaeologists were "doctors of the dead". When I pointed out that his nickname for my profession didn't make any sense, it only seemed to make it funnier to him.

The coolness of the basement studio didn't prevent me from perspiring profusely as I pried the front of the box off with the enthusiasm of a kid on Christmas morning. Finally, it fell like the draw bridge of a castle; packing material cascading onto the floor, revealing the crate's contents. It happened so quickly, the sight of it startled me.

A dark angel stared out from the inside of the crate, perched in such a manner that it seemed as if it was prepared to leap and fly away. Dark, not just because it was formed from a stone as black as a cloud of smoke, but because its wings were those of a bat. Its ears rose high and pointy, surrounding a head that was gaunt and malformed, looking more like a skull than a face.

When I caught my breath, I noticed that the thing was crouching upon some sort of pedestal. Cautiously, almost as if not to frighten it, I approached the statue to marvel at its sinister detail. I found myself mesmerized, frozen and staring into the abyss where its eyes should have been. Then I realized the eyes were indeed there, glistening so darkly that I could see myself in them.

Stepping back to view my gift in its entirety, I began to appreciate the reason Bob had sent this for my birthday. The creature sat perched on a tall, square block that held a chiseled inscription. A few of the characters were instantly recognizable, but spread among far too many that were not. An ancient puzzle to solve... I loved it.

Part of me wanted to laugh at how great a gift it was, and how Bob knew the four guardian angels had no value to me in comparison to this magnificent, stone beast. The other part of me held back my joy, feeling as if it would be almost disrespectful to my morbid guest. I only wish some part of me could have remembered, no matter how well-intentioned Bob was in his efforts to make me enjoy life, how I always found myself getting into trouble as a result.

When Bob said "See you soon," that usually meant about two months. It had taken the crate almost three weeks to arrive, so I had about five weeks to solve my birthday gift before he returned, near the end of October.

I'm not sure if I slept at all during that first week, re-reading the books in my library to refresh my knowledge of lost civilizations and the occult, and consuming volumes of new research in an effort to translate the inscription. The language was similar to ancient Hebrew dialects I had come across, with elements of dead Eastern characters, often grouped together as that of the Magi. Still other characters I cross-referenced with that of the Etruscan texts recently found in northern Italy.

The fragments of words I deciphered made little sense. G-O-L was the beginning of the large inscription, but the stone base was quite weathered, making it nearly impossible to discern some of the markings. Below that were etched words such as blood, servant and master. After close to a month, I had hit a wall of frustration as imposing as the monolith itself.

Long, sleepless nights of constant work didn't make the task any easier. At times, the draftiness of my studio made me feel the creature was sighing in impatience. Its eyes, those unblinking obsidian orbits, followed me around the room as if the thing were waiting for me to unlock its secret. Falling asleep from sheer exhaustion, I would awaken to the sound of grinding stone pushing its mass across the cold, damp slab of the studio. And on the rare occurrence when the room was in total darkness, I would think it was moving, so slightly, like an enormous, restless sloth in a cage.

But in the light of day, and when clear of mind, it was just the graven image of a fallen angel.

I awoke on this night, the night of my death, with my head resting on my drawing table, having scribbled for the thousandth time the letters and words of the inscription. I stirred suddenly, sensing a cold presence, as if something were standing behind me and looking over my shoulder. I turned and saw the creature perched where it had been since its arrival. When I turned back to the table, the sound of grinding stone gripped me. My neck was rigid with fear, and I was terrified to look back again. I moved just enough to see a murky reflection in a picture frame, and through it, the soulless black eyes of the creature looked back at me.

With my heart pounding, I spun around wildly and prepared to scream for help. Nothing. There it stood as always, staring back at me with a cold, emotionless gaze.

From deep inside came the answer, like a maniacal revelation. I knew what it was. G-O-L and the other indistinguishable characters—a golem. This wasn't the image of a fallen angel Bob found in the holy land. It was a golem, a creature that, according to legend, was chiseled from stone or molded from clay and could be animated by a magical invocation to do its master's bidding. All the fragmented words suddenly begin to make sense. I knew enough to assume what the other characters stood for, and what the words meant.

GOLEM —Let Blood Bind Servant To Master.

I was electrified with my own maddening genius. Then the realization that this was no mere puzzle, this was a golem. I pricked my thumb and began scribbling in my own blood. I copied the inscription character-for-character on a piece of paper, and took my place in front of the inanimate idol. Could I actually bring this creature to life?

As I stood in front of it, its stare hypnotized me. In my mind, I heard the stone moving, saw its head tilting, and its mouth open. I shut my eyes and shook my head, and when I opened them again, there it stood as it had been.

I took heart from my vision and stepped closer, placing the paper in the creature's mouth.

And then death gripped me.

The golem's eyes stared blankly into mine as its stone appendages came to life. Its wings unfolded and reached out over me, its talons impaling my hands, spreading my arms away from me and lifting me off the studio floor. With a grating sound, it stepped from its perch, and as it did, the thing lifted me further above it. Its movement was a grinding yet fluid motion. Then it pulled me closer, enfolding me within its wings, staring at me with its dead, black eyes.

Its left hand seized my throat and its right hand slashed open my chest. The creature closed its mouth on the bloodstained paper, then spat it out against my face.

This thing was no golem. I now experienced the true revelation, the one free of madness and pure with the knowledge I had long forgotten. The word I so eagerly accepted as GOLEM was in reality GOLGOTH, the Angel of Torment.

I can see myself dying in the reflection of its eyes. The creature's unrelenting grip around my throat allows me no last breath. "Let Blood Bind Servant To Master," the meaning of the cryptic message was clear to me now, even as my vision blurred; it was not what my power-mad mind wanted it to be. Sheer dread swept over me, as my final mortal thought was that of how my suffering would serve to nourish my newly resurrected master.

# SPIDERS IN THE ATTIC

*by Joseph Vargo*

Pale moonlight filtered into Anna's bedroom window through the silken mesh of her curtains, casting web-like patterns on the hardwood floor. The autumn moon danced behind the clouds, appearing again and again to illuminate the darkened heavens. As she lay awake in bed, Anna drifted between the mundane reality of her adolescent life and a realm of gothic dreams and fantasies. Outside the wind whistled though the barren branches, rustling the few remaining leaves that had not yet withered and fallen. As she began to return to her dreams, another sound roused her from her sleep. Between the howls of the cool autumn breeze, she heard a voice that sounded as if it had faintly whispered her name.

"Anna..."

She listened more intently, but there was only wind to be heard. After a few minutes her eyelids grew heavy and she began drifting back to the land of dreams when she heard the voice call her name once more.

"Anna..."

She sat up and slowly crept out of bed, then began to step as silently as possible toward her window. She peered cautiously through the curtains to survey her yard. The moonlight fell upon the barren trees, casting long shadows that appeared to reach out with bony fingers across the ground, straining to catch the fallen leaves that rustled past. Clouds obscured the moon once again and

Anna now noticed a dim glow emanating from the attic window of the abandoned house next to her home. She drew back the curtain and stared into the darkness and as she did, the light went out, as if someone had suddenly extinguished a candle.

Anna stepped back behind the curtain and continued to watch the house for the next several hours, until the crimson rays of sunlight announced the approaching dawn. Finally, she returned to her bed and fell fast asleep to dream once more of ravens and vampire lords. Late in the afternoon, she awoke to the sound of her stepfather banging on her bedroom door, yelling at her to get out of bed.

Since it was a Saturday, Anna had no school, leaving her with the entire weekend to investigate the abandoned house. When she asked her mother if someone had moved in next door, she replied "No," without stopping to question her. Anna dropped the subject and didn't mention anything about what she had seen the night before, fearful that her parents would try to thwart her from investigating further. It seemed that they always tried to stop her from doing anything remotely dangerous or fun.

As her parents became lost in their daily routines, Anna slipped out of her house and made her way next door. She approached the decrepit old house and stood before it, surveying every window for signs of life. The old Colonial-style home didn't look like particularly frightening, yet something about it made her pause before proceeding closer. Hesitantly, she climbed the old wooden porch steps and peered in through the tall window beside the front door.

The interior of the house was completely devoid of furniture and there were no apparent signs of life to be seen. Weak sunlight filtered in through the window, illuminating thick motes of dust. Anna tested the latch to see if it was locked, and to her surprise the door opened.

Glancing around to make sure no one was watching, Anna quickly entered the home, thrilled and frightened at the same time. She closed the heavy door behind her and leaned against it. Other than the stale smell that permeated the interior of the house, nothing seemed out of the ordinary. A quick survey of the other rooms led her to the conclusion that the house was empty. Anna began to wonder if she had simply let her wild imagination get the better of her. Just then she became aware of a creaking noise from the floor above her. As silently as possible, she made her way up the attic stairs.

She lightly placed her fingertips upon the attic door and slowly pushed it open as quietly as possible. The old attic was strewn with cobwebs that hung like tattered drapes from the support beams and cascaded down to cover the walls. With her first step into the room, she could feel that the attic was much colder than the rest of the house, cold enough to make her shiver. At the far side of the attic, an antique rocking chair faced the window overlooking Anna's home. The rocker swayed slightly, as if someone had recently been sitting in it.

As Anna advanced across the dusty floorboards, she now noticed a half-melted candle resting in a candle holder on the windowsill. She crept toward the old chair to discover a crackled porcelain doll lying in the dust. She picked it up and recognized the doll as one that had belonged to her when she was a child. Her hands began to tremble and the doll slipped from her grasp, dropping to the floor.

A sudden chill swept over her and she was overtaken with the uneasy feeling that she was being watched. In the periphery of her vision, she perceived a dark shape lurking behind a thick layer of cobwebs to her right.

"Who's there?" Anna whispered into the darkness. But the shadow made no sound. Anna brushed her hand through the webbing that obscured her view and suddenly realized that what she had first taken to be cobwebs were in reality spiderwebs. Dozens of large black spiders came scampering out of the opening she had made in the veil of webs. They flooded out onto the floor and swarmed over the broken doll at her feet. Anna screamed and jumped back, then she turned her gaze to the darkness above her. The entire attic was infested with nests, and hundreds of spiders were crawling across the ceiling directly over her head.

Anna screamed again then ran out of the house, frantically swiping her hands over her hair and body to brush away any spiders. She burst through the front door and out into the yard. Anna shuddered as she looked back up at the attic window but there were no traces of mystery intruders or swarming spiders to be seen. Still trembling, she hurried home to the sanctuary of her bedroom and locked the door behind her.

Later that night, Anna found herself wandering inside the land of dreams once again, but the landscape that surrounded her was now strangely familiar. She was back in the attic of the abandoned house, but her view was altered, as if she were observing the scene from a higher perspective. The dusty floor was now a mesh of webs, not unlike the pattern of shadows that were cast nightly upon her own bedroom floor. The rest of the room was pitch black.

A strange buzzing noise emanated from somewhere in the darkness and Anna took a step toward the sound to investigate its source. As she began to move, she now noticed that she had the long, spindly legs of a spider, which enabled her to crawl along the web of shadows that covered the room. As Anna drew near the buzzing sound, she could see an enormous fly caught in the confines of the web. As she crept closer, the insect shrieked and flailed wildly, but was unable to free itself. For a long moment she stared into the honeycomb pattern that covered the fly's glowing red eyes, transfixed by her own reflection—a reflection which revealed her own form to be that of a giant black widow spider. Without further hesitation, she quickly advanced upon her trapped prey and began to weave a suffocating net of webbing around it to muffle its shrieks. She climbed on top of the helpless fly and tore into its abdomen with her fangs, injecting her deadly venom into the the writhing creature and drinking its blood.

Anna awoke in a fevered sweat, her young heart pounding. Sitting up in bed, she peered out of her window into the dead of night. Once again, a candle was burning in the attic window of the house next door. A moment later, she heard the voice call her name, just as it had the night before, and as if under a hypnotic spell, she heeded the beckoning call. Wearing only her nightgown, she snuck out of her house.

She made her way into the spider house and up the attic stairs. When she reached the top, the attic door opened with a creak. A flickering glow emanated from the opposite side of the attic. Anna paused for a moment, allowing her eyes to adjust to the gloom, then slowly stepped toward the dim light. Across the room, a hunched figure sat in the rocking chair, silhouetted by the auburn candle glow.

An old woman sat in the rocking chair, swaying rhythmically back and forth. At the old hag's feet, a young boy lay bound and gagged by thin silken cords that tied his wrists to his ankles. The old woman turned her gaze toward Anna and spoke to her in a gravelly voice.

"Welcome my dear."

Anna stood frozen in place as the old crone continued speaking. "I've been watching you for quite a while...patiently, silently, watching and waiting. Now the time has come for me to guide you. Your parents don't understand you, and they never will. They still treat you as a child. But they can't even begin to imagine the things you're capable of." As the old woman spoke, Anna felt strangely at ease and an eerie calm swept over her.

"Come closer, my dear."

Anna had lost all will to resist. She glanced down at the captive boy again. His eyes conveyed a desperate plea for help. He reminded her of a fly caught in a spider's web. Anna returned her gaze to the old woman and took a step toward her. The crone leaned forward out of the shadows. The woman's face was withered and wrinkled, and her eyes were glazed with cataracts. Her flesh was pale, but her lips were a deep glistening red.

"Who are you?" Anna whispered.

The old crone leaned in close to Anna's face and whispered, "We are one and the same, you and I. We are the widows of the web."

Anna slowly began to take notice of a legion of ghastly faces peering out of the shadows behind the mesh of spiderwebs on either side of her. As her eyes finally became accustomed to the darkness, she could see several skeletons tied to the attic's support beams, covered with webs and spiders.

The old woman spoke again, "There is much work to be done. All I ask is that you stay with me and allow me to guide you. Stay with me Anna," the crone whispered, "Anna... Anna..."

"Anna," The young nurse called her name again, "Anna, can you hear me?" But the old lady didn't respond. Instead, she sat in her rocking chair, transfixed upon the spiderweb in the corner of her window. A fly struggled to free itself from the web as a large black spider descended upon it. A smile formed on the old woman's crackled face as she watched the spider devour its prey.

A husky male orderly entered the psychiatric wardroom and offered his advice to the nurse. "It's no use, she won't speak to anyone. As far as I know, she hasn't uttered a word in all the years she's been here."

"Why the restraints?" She asked, glancing down at the thick leather manacles that bound the old woman to her chair.

"Just a precaution," the orderly whispered, then continued in a hushed tone, "The police found her in the attic of her home, surrounded by dead bodies that she had bound and tied to the rafters. We call her the Black Widow. She killed her entire family and anyone else who wandered into her parlor. She poisoned them all, then kept their bodies tied up in her attic as macabre mementos. She lived in that old house for nearly sixty years before the police finally discovered her."

"She doesn't talk, she just sits there. Who knows what goes on inside her head. If you ask me, I say the old bird's still got a few spiders in the attic." He laughed at his own pun, but the nurse didn't crack a smile.

"It's actually very sad," the nurse replied. "She'll never leave this place."

But Anna didn't hear their words. She had already returned to the morbid dreamworld of her youth where her mind wandered free and unrestrained by the reality of her physical bonds. Spiders crawled across her hands and she lifted them high, laughing and dancing, twirling off into the shadows of her twisted imagination.

LE JOUR DE GLOIRE EST ARRIVÉ

# BROTHERHOOD OF SHADOWS

*by Joseph Iorillo*

"Let us raise our glasses, gentlemen, to Professor Harris Logan, soon to be the newest Master of the Seventeenth Degree," declared Clive Yardley, who stood at the head of the table, wine glass in hand. The other Masters also rose, lifting their glasses, and the soft, opulent glow from the chandeliers twinkled off the crystal glasses and the polished sterling silverware like silent fireworks.

Harris Logan, despite his cynicism and mistrust, found himself smiling and blushing. He had never been the subject of a laudatory toast before—and certainly not in the company of such men. Not only was Clive Yardley a long-time Master of the Seventeenth Degree, he was also a high-ranking vice president of Drayfort & Drayfort, one of the wealthiest private equity firms in London. To Logan's right stood Geoffrey Parmentier, the chief advisor to the French Minister of Defense. Up and down the table, all these Masters of the Seventeenth Degree emanated affluence and influence, confidence and power—and here they were, toasting Harris Logan.

"Thank you," he murmured, his throat suddenly very dry. He had meant to say something more profound and memorable but in the presence of the Brotherhood's highest level of Masters he found himself as abashed as a schoolboy.

To Logan's left, Michael Mansfield patted Harris on the back and winked. "You're doing fine," Mansfield whispered.

"This is Professor Logan's first trip to England," Yardley explained to the other Masters, "and I'm sure he's a bit jet-lagged and a bit intimidated by being surrounded by so many new faces. But rest assured, Mr. Logan, we are all friends here. Your friends. If the Brotherhood teaches us anything it's that you will always have us to rely upon, without question."

"Hear hear," someone affirmed.

Logan's smile was polite but wary. He was waiting for the catch. There was always a catch.

Yardley smiled, his eyes brimming with nostalgia. "I can remember when I was in your place. Years and years ago. The Ritual of the Crossing had taken a lot out of me and, I admit, I would have been content to stay a Master of the Sixteenth Degree." He chuckled and feigned a horrific shudder. "After the Crossing, I thought, No more. Keep me at Sixteen. Hell, drop me back down to Fifteen—at least that was just a written test! Those were the days, weren't they?"

"Yes," Logan said, "they were." The initiation into the Fifteenth Degree was indeed a written exam concerning the history and philosophic underpinnings of the Brotherhood of Shadows and Light. The questions were at first routine and factual, quizzing the initiate on the founding of the group in medieval France as a secretive conclave of radical philosophers and thinkers who were unimpressed with Church teachings. The questions then dealt with the Brotherhood's subsequent persecution by the Church as a heretical, even diabolical sect practicing Satanic rites. Eventually, though, the questions became more introspective. One question was, What is the purpose of the Brotherhood?

After all his years in the group, Logan could answer that without much hesitation. To perfect the human being by lifting him out of the world of animal instinct and instilling in him new instincts of trust and faith.

"It's quite profound, when you think about it," Mansfield had once told him over brandy at a restaurant near Mansfield's law firm in Chicago several years ago. "Most of our lives are spent reacting to things based on our primal needs, our selfish desires, our fight-or-flight instincts. Which is fine—if you want to remain on a level with animals who think only about food and self-preservation. But aren't we capable of much more than that?"

"If a man is robbing you at knifepoint, a good fight-or-flight response isn't something to sneeze at."

"No, but that's my point. The world as it's constructed keeps us at the animal level. Thieves rob out of a primal lust for power, or because they're hungry and desperate. Their victims cower like rabbits and let themselves be robbed, hoping not to be harmed. And at those moments there is little that separates us from the primitive, fearful hominids that foraged for food half a million years ago."

"And the Brotherhood hopes to change that," Logan said, trying not to sound too skeptical. Being skeptical, however, was what made him the University of Chicago's most effective professor of philosophy.

Now, as the gathered Masters of the Seventeenth Degree sipped their wine and listened to Yardley, Grand Master and Protector of the Royal Secret, Logan tried to quell his slowly mounting anxiety at the initiation ritual to come. He took a long drink of the pinot noir and tried not to think about the Ritual of the Crossing. That had been more than a year ago, and he still occasionally had nightmares about it.

"This is a monumental night for you, Mr. Logan," Yardley said, beaming. "Tonight, all your years of fellowship in the Brotherhood will crystallize into your official rebirth as a Perfected Master, and you too will be able to wear the Ring of Seventeen." He held up his right hand. On the ring finger was the familiar silver band encrusted with seventeen small sapphires. The chandeliers' light glinted off similar rings on the hands of the other Masters. "A petty material token, to be sure, but one that symbolizes your spiritual evolution under our care. You have traveled from the shadows, from the ordinary human realm of mistrust, self-interest and fear and arrived, finally, at the light. During the Ritual of the Final Secret, you will have in your hands the ultimate truth to which we are all privy. The one you have heard whispers about all these years. The secret that has undoubtedly been a source of much speculation within you."

Logan said nothing, even though the eyes of the Masters seemed to study him more keenly than before.

"It's all right," Yardley said. "The promise of the secret is a key motivator for many in the lower degrees. Everyone wants the revelation and the power it holds. But, really, your tenure here in the Brotherhood and your spiritual progress through the ranks has revealed the secret to you already. You have learned all the lessons we had to teach, and our knowledge is now your knowledge, whether you realize it consciously or not. Nevertheless, you will hold in your hands the Final Secret. And once the ritual is complete, we shall toast your rebirth and have a proper celebration."

"Do you still have that bottle of thirty-year-old scotch?" Mansfield asked. "The single-malt?"

Yardley laughed. "I most certainly do, and we'll all have a taste. No better way to celebrate a rebirthday, eh?" The Grand Master nodded to the others, and almost simultaneously they begin donning their scarlet robes, which the small platoon of footmen and underbutlers had begun distributing.

Logan was the only member of the group not given a robe. He felt curiously naked in his business suit. He was startled when one of the Masters began patting him down and removing the contents of Logan's various pockets.

"What are you doing?"

The Master did not answer but merely smiled.

Yardley clapped Logan reassuringly on the shoulder. "Not feeling nervous, are you?"

"No," Logan said, clearing his throat.

"Of course he's not," Mansfield said. "He's not one of those dreadful First or Second Degreers. He's made of stronger stuff than that."

"One hour and it will all be over," Yardley said. "Not a thing to worry about."

"The irony is that it's the easiest ritual of all of them," someone said as they moved to the back stairwell that led down to the cellar. There was a small antique service elevator, but Logan had explained that he would rather take the stairs; his mild claustrophobia made even roomy limousines seem like coffins. Yardley's mansion was overwhelmingly large, and the winding stone stairwell corkscrewed into the earth for what seemed like half a mile. Finally, they reached the dank wine cellar, which was lit by several medieval wall sconces that held flaming torches.

The Masters of the Seventeenth Degree, laughing and chatting about recent rare vintages up for auction, led Logan through the rows of dusty bottles until they came to what appeared to be an oblong altar covered with a black sheet.

Logan's heart pounded. He tried to steady his breathing.

The Masters fanned out around the altar. Yardley stood behind it, in the middle, reminding Logan of Jesus in da Vinci's "Last Supper." Logan noticed an object on the altar—a small, tattered canvas scroll bound with a black ribbon.

"This is the Secret," Yardley said. "And it will be yours for one hour."

Logan's mouth was dry. After eleven years, here it was, just a few inches from his hand.

"But again, Mr. Logan," Yardley said, "its contents have already been divulged to you in one way or another by your time in the Brotherhood. What have you heard about the Secret?"

"Just rumors."

"What sort of rumors?" Parmentier asked, his thin lips twisting into a wry smile.

"That the Secret deals with the true origin of man. Or that it reveals the location of some source of wealth that would put El Dorado to shame."

The Masters exchanged unreadable looks. "What else?" Yardley asked.

"That those who learn it end up with worldly success beyond their fondest imaginings." Logan met Yardley's amused gaze. He knew that once Yardley had passed the Ritual of the Final Secret his net worth quadrupled; Logan also knew that another Master, Lewis Benning, had progressed from an unremarkable professor of political theory to a key advisor on the President's national security team once he had gone through the rite.

In an hour Logan would be one of them. His hands ached to unfurl the scroll.

"Perhaps that success had more to do with the accumulated power of all the Brotherhood's teachings," Yardley countered, "and nothing to do with this." He laid a finger on the scroll.

"And if the Secret really has no power or magic, then you wouldn't need to have it guarded day and night by armed men."

Yardley's eyebrows rose. A smile slowly erupted on his face. "You have certainly been a most intrepid investigator, Mr. Logan." The Grand Master nodded to another man, who presented Logan with two books of matches.

Logan's brow furrowed. "What are these for?"

Yardley blinked. "It gets dark in the coffin."

"Coffin," Logan said, not understanding.

With a flourish, Yardley removed the black sheet from the altar, revealing the stone sarcophagus beneath. Upon the lid was a relief of a fallen knight, his arms crossed over his armored chest, the effigy of a scroll clasped in his hands. Logan noticed the words carved along the rim of the lid: *Le jour de gloire est arrivé* (the day of glory has arrived).

All eyes of the Masters were upon Logan, who was perspiring heavily, even though the cellar was damp and cool.

"Do you have faith in our words, in the words of your Brothers and Masters?" asked Geoffrey Parmentier.

"Yes," Logan said after a brief hesitation. Images of the Ritual of the Crossing flashed through his mind, but he tried to banish them.

"Do you trust in our words?" asked another man, an elderly gentleman named Gustafson.

"Yes," Logan said.

"Do you have faith in our honesty, in our integrity, in the words of our teachings?" asked Yardley.

"You keep asking the same thing in different ways," Logan said, becoming slightly annoyed. "Yes, I do have faith."

Yardley handed him the scroll, a gentle, pained look on his face. "Then you won't need this."

The scroll felt warm in Logan's hand. He could feel the centuries of power within it, as if it were some pulsing, living thing. He was about to undo the black ribbon tying the canvas when Mansfield stopped him.

"Not yet."

Six of the other Masters took hold of the sarcophagus' massive granite lid and lifted it away. The casket's interior was decorated with elaborate carved diagrams and words that Logan could barely make out in the dim light.

"Just as our founder, Henri le Dechambeau, lay for days in a tomb, buried alive by the Inquisition with only the sacred teachings of the Brotherhood for comfort, so too will you lay in this tomb," Yardley said. "And just as our founder was rescued by his Brothers, who overpowered Church gendarmes, so too shall we be your salvation. We will come for you in one hour. Lie still and remember that you already know the Secret, Mr. Logan. It is within you already." He nodded to the sarcophagus. "Get in."

I can do this, Logan thought. He took a deep breath and let it out. His sweaty hands gripped the rolled canvas and his head rang with the echo of the heavy stone lid being dropped back into place above him. He was trapped in total darkness. Logan's sense of claustrophobia was threatening to blossom into full-blown panic and hyperventilation, but he forced himself to calm down. This was too important. Like the carved knight above him, he held the Secret. It was his.

The Master who had spoken earlier was right—this did seem to be the easiest of all the seventeen rituals. It was certainly easier than the horror of the Crossing.

And yet at first he had thought the Ritual of the Crossing would be an easy one as well. On that day fifteen months ago, when the Brotherhood determined that Logan was ready, one of the Masters of the Sixteenth Degree presented him with a crude schematic diagram of what appeared to be a wooden bridge, with many of the planks missing.

"It would be helpful," the Master said, smiling, "if you would familiarize yourself with this. Where to step and where not to step."

Logan assumed that the Ritual would be much like many of the other initiation rites. The Brothers would take him and the other Sixteenth Degree initiates to one of the Brotherhood's luxurious lodges, there would be a stylized ritual or innocuous puzzle to solve in one of the back rooms, and then they would all have drinks and cigars. Not that he didn't take the Ritual seriously—he did. Passing it was another step toward the Secret. For the two weeks prior to the Ritual, Logan studied the diagram, trying in vain to memorize the locations of the missing planks.

It wasn't until two days before the rite that it dawned on him that the missing boards had a pattern. That pattern was music.

While he was idly humming the Brotherhood's official anthem, "In the Darkest Hour There is Light," Logan was struck by the realization that the song's meter was mirrored in the bridge's diagram. Whole notes were a sequence of four missing planks, half notes were two, quarter notes were one. The entire first verse of the song played out throughout the entire hundred-yard span of the bridge. Jubilant, Logan had been tempted to share his gestalt with the other two initiates—Meyer, an overweight, melancholic accountant, and Newsome, a quiet but sarcastic film studio executive—but he kept it to himself.

On the night of the ritual, Logan was so confident and happy that he slapped Meyer on the back and told the glum accountant several off-color jokes to take his mind off the rite—which would, Logan was sure, consist of the initiates having to draw the diagram of the bridge from memory, like some strange SAT test.

When the Masters of the Sixteenth Degree blindfolded the three initiates and loaded them into the back of three limousines, however, Logan's exultation quickly faded. When he felt the car climbing higher and higher, advancing up onto what felt like mountain roads, Logan's heart began throbbing in panic.

As the three men were herded out of the limousines, the icy wind whipped violently at their clothes. Logan chanced a quick peek under his blindfold and was horrified to see that they were at the edge of a cliff that dropped nearly two hundred feet to a roaring, twisting, boulder-strewn river below. A dilapidated bridge stretched nearly a hundred yards across the chasm, with many of the planks missing. The screaming wind rocked the bridge back and forth like a hammock.

Logan felt like he was going to throw up.

"In the Year of Our Lord 1322," said one of the Sixteenth Degree Masters, raising his voice to be heard over the winter gale, "our founder, Henri le Dechambeau, was chased by the Church's armed militia across a bridge in Amiens, a bridge which miraculously held steady for him but disintegrated under the feet of his pursuers."

Logan could feel one of the Masters take his elbow and guide him to the entrance to the footbridge. He could hear the bridge rattle and creak.

"Initiates into the Sixteenth Degree of the Brotherhood of Shadows and Light," said another Master, "your task tonight as honest Brothers and Knights of Perfect Truth is to answer a question I will put forth to you. Mr. Meyer, please step forward."

Logan could hear the scrape of Meyer's reluctant footsteps.

"Mr. Meyer, Accomplished Master of the Fifteenth Degree, do you wish to replicate our founder's crossing on that fateful night in 1322?"

Meyer cleared his throat and said hoarsely, "Yes. I will."

"Then step onto the bridge, dear Brother, and may the Universal Power deliver you safely to the other side."

Logan didn't risk another peek under his blindfold, but he heard it all. He heard Meyer's frightened panting, the creak of the bridge, the scream of the wind, and the halting, erratic clop-clop of Meyer's shoes groping for purchase on the planks. Logan heard Meyer's gasping yelp as he stumbled and nearly dropped through one of the gaps in the planking. Logan's heart raced as if he were the one on the bridge. When he heard Meyer's sobbing cries, Logan himself wanted to cry. Eventually the shriek of the wind drowned out Meyer's voice, but Logan remembered hearing the man stumble again. Logan heard what sounded like a man's hands grappling for handholds on the planks, then, a moment later, Logan heard the distinct splash in the rough waters below.

Logan fell to his knees and vomited. One of the Masters helped him back to his feet.

The Master asked him softly, "Mr. Logan, Accomplished Master of the Fifteenth Degree, do you wish to replicate our founder's crossing on that fateful night in 1322?"

"Yes," he found himself saying in an unsteady voice, "I will."

The Master tightened Logan's blindfold and pushed him gently onto the bridge. He made his first few steps with agonizing slowness, humming the Brotherhood's anthem under his breath.

In the darkest hour, there is light—

The light of holy truth—

He did not stumble. With every dreaded whole note, he stopped before the four missing boards and braced himself. Then he leapt, nearly weeping with relief when his feet touched down on solid wood again. The wind roared like a raging lion and his hands were nearly frostbitten as they gripped the frayed rope handrails for support. Seventy-five yards… fifty yards… thirty… and then, toward the end of the first verse, a measure with two consecutive whole notes. That translated into eight missing boards. Since each plank seemed to feel a little less than a foot wide, that meant he was facing nearly an eight-foot jump.

If he got even a slight running start, he could do it. He gingerly backed up a few feet, mindful of the one missing plank behind him, then took a deep breath. The wind rocked the bridge. I can do this, he thought. He hummed the song, thinking of nothing but the Secret, which was that much closer now. He could do this.

We know that truth will triumph

In the hour of darkest night…

He bit his lip and leapt. That was when his luck seemed to run out. The wind shook the bridge yet again, making it groan and undulate like a boa constrictor. He was airborne but the sudden movement of the bridge meant he had no way of knowing if his landing spot would still be there.

Please, God, please.

He landed awkwardly on the planks, and he pitched to the side, nearly spilling over the edge into the icy water. Logan grabbed the rope handrails and hauled himself to his feet again, gasping. He had done it. He screamed in triumph. There was only a short section left to traverse, and adrenaline and confidence propelled him easily to the other side. The feel of the solid earth and brittle, frozen grass made him cry out again in ecstasy. He tore off the blindfold and saw the Masters on the other side applauding him.

"I did it!" Logan cried. He was so happy that he forgot about Meyer. Logan felt so good that he rushed back across the bridge to his Brothers. It was much easier now that he could see the gaps in the planking illuminated by the half moon.

Back safely on the other side, the Masters congratulated him and welcomed him to the Sixteenth Degree.

Then it was Newsome's turn.

One of the Masters solemnly asked Newsome the ritualistic question: did he wish to replicate the Brotherhood's crossing on the fateful night in 1322?

To Logan's surprise, he heard Newsome chuckle and say, "No, not really."

Newsome's answer was not nearly as surprising as what the Master said next.

"Congratulations, Brother Newsome, and welcome to the Sixteenth Degree."

Before everyone went back to the waiting limousines, Logan took aside one of the Masters. "I don't understand. How could he be admitted to this level? He didn't make the crossing like I did."

The Master blinked at him. "You could have said no."

Logan stared at him, not comprehending.

"You weren't paying close enough attention," the Master said. "Your task was not to make the crossing but merely to tell us if you wanted to cross. That was all."

Stunned, Logan looked behind him at the bridge writhing and rattling in the unforgiving wind. "Meyer," he said. "He's dead, isn't he? You let him die."

The Master's eyebrows rose. "Mr. Logan, the Brotherhood never harms its Brothers."

"He fell. He drowned. Or he was killed on the rocks. We all heard him —"

The Master smiled. "You heard something. But have you ever stopped to consider that it might have been a bit of misdirection? That Mr. Meyer was actually a plant we placed here tonight to keep you and Mr. Newsome a bit off balance? In your excitement at crossing the bridge, did you stop to count the number of Brothers on this side?"

Logan peered into the darkness at the retreating Masters, most of whom were already ensconced in the waiting limousines. "I know what I heard," Logan said weakly.

The Master squeezed Logan's shoulder. "You trust too much in your senses, in your instincts. Sometimes they can be wrong."

And sometimes, Logan thought, laying in the warm blackness of the ritual coffin, they can be right. His instincts kept him in the Brotherhood even though there was much about the group that confused him and made him uncomfortable. His instincts told him that these men, despite their quietness and their shunning of the spotlight, possessed a power that elevated them above the rest of humanity. And at long last, Logan held that power, that Final Secret, in his hands.

Lie still and remember that you already know the Secret.

But he couldn't do that. In one hour the Masters would come and they would take the Secret away from him. He pressed upward on the heavy lid to test its weight but even putting all his strength into the effort he could not budge it. Out of breath, Logan thought about the knight carved on the lid. Was the warrior meant to be sleeping, or was he dead?

Sleeping, you idiot. Dechambeau had been rescued by his Brothers. Logan mustn't start scaring himself.

Breathing heavily in the muggy, close air, he undid the black ribbon and unrolled the scroll. He groped for one of the matchbooks in his suit pocket. It was hard to maneuver in the coffin but he clumsily managed to strike a match. The brief, flickering fire showed him a tantalizing glimpse of the Secret: a circle of dozens of indecipherable symbols on an otherwise empty piece of canvas. The stream of symbols spiraled inward to the center of the scroll like a serpent's tail.

The match burned down close to his fingertips and he shook it out. In those few seconds, however, Logan saw the carved symbols on the underside of the sarcophagus' lid. He struck another match and peered at them more closely, running his fingers over the strange sigils. They comprised the familiar pictographic code that

Dechambeau and his early followers used to communicate with one another without the Church learning their secrets. The symbols were arranged in neat rows, with English equivalents next to each character. The coffin's lid had been imprinted with a miniature dictionary of complete words—like air, fire, water and earth—while the sides of the sarcophagus had been chiseled with translations of individual letters and numbers. Although the stuffy air and lack of ventilation had made Logan sodden with perspiration, he smiled. He had been an attentive student of the Brotherhood's history and knew many parts of the code by heart. But time was running out; he estimated that he had about forty-five minutes before the Masters of the Seventeenth Degree fetched him.

Using a pencil stub he dug out of another jacket pocket, he jotted down the translation of the spiral of symbols on the interior of one of the matchbooks. Logan was a methodical, consistent man; he would begin at the beginning and work his way toward the center of the spiral. The matches, however, were a source of frustration. They burned only for a few seconds, a painfully short window for him to scan the interior of the stone casket.

Those who crave... His sweaty fingers were trembling, and sweat stung his eyes as he wrote the words. He mustn't lose his head. Each matchbook contained about twenty matches. He couldn't afford to waste their light. Logan had to make sure each burst of flame allowed him to translate some portion of the Secret. But his breathing was becoming more and more labored and he felt dizzy. One of the matches became so moist with sweat that he was unable to light it. When he finally got another flame going, his bleary eyes had difficulty focusing and the fire burned out before he could translate the next chunk of the message.

Get control of yourself, he told himself. Solve the problem.

He took in a deep, gasping breath and carefully struck another match. Instead of translating the message in order and risk being stumped on a word or letter, he decided to simply translate whatever section of the Secret seemed easiest, so long as he made progress with every matchstrike.

Those who crave... deserve... forty... air... here... accomplished master...

Coughing and trying to shake off an ever-strengthening wave of fatigue that was tugging at him, Logan nevertheless couldn't keep himself from smiling. Much of the message was falling into place. He might actually translate the entire Secret before the Masters came.

... power the most... least... cubic... slightly more than sixty...

His heart felt a surge of adrenaline. The numbers could signify longitude and latitude—perhaps the location of some artifact, some treasure? The lower degrees of the Brotherhood were awash with rumors about some unimaginably enormous hidden source of wealth.

Those who crave power the most... lies...degree...

Logan coughed, striking another match. He translated a few more pieces of the puzzle: every... minute... The flame burned down to his fingertips and he shook it out. He was in darkness again. The air in the sarcophagus was as muggy as a sauna. He undid the top button of his shirt. He went to tear another match from the matchbook but it was empty. He had one matchbook left.

Logan flexed his fingers and carefully lit another match. His ears were ringing and his ragged breath sounded like a sluggish breeze passing over dead leaves. Some of the symbols were not entire words but strings of individual letters. A... R... R... I... L... O... N...

Another match sizzled to life, and Logan jotted down a few more letters. Then he blinked. As the flame guttered and died, he realized he was staring at his own name. Harris Logan.

What's going on?

His fingers were cramping from lighting so many matches, but he forced himself to continue. His heart thundered in his chest. Flames burst to life and then died, and the words fell into place on the inside of the sweat-stained matchbook. And then suddenly it was over. He had translated the entire Secret.

*Those who crave power the most deserve it the least.*

*The coffin contains thirty cubic feet of air, enough for slightly more than sixty minutes of sustainable life. Every match consumes nearly a minute's worth of this air.*

*May the Universal Power grant you deliverance from the bonds of this world.*

*Here lies Harris Logan, Accomplished Master of the Sixteenth Degree.*

The light went out and Logan found himself in darkness again, lying amid more than thirty spent matches. With his shoulder, he strained against the sarcophagus' lid, but it refused to budge. He pounded on it, screaming. "Can anyone hear me? Hello? Let me out!" His voice ricocheted against the stone walls of the coffin.

The Brotherhood never harms its Brothers, the Master had told him at the bridge. Of course they didn't—they just let the Brothers do it to themselves. Logan laughed miserably, finally dissolving into painful, gasping sobs. He began screaming again, screaming until he was hoarse, until he had no voice left.

# AFRAID OF THE DARK

*by Joseph Vargo*

The hollow was deathly still as the three teens sat around the sinister glow of the Jack-o-lantern, telling ghost stories on Halloween night. The flickering candle cast eerie shadows from the middle of the fire pit, causing strange shapes to writhe and slither across the boys faces. Rob had just finished telling his story about the escaped serial killer with a hook for a hand. He ended the tale with a dramatic yell as he lunged toward Kevin, making him scream and topple backward off the log he was sitting on. The third boy, Greg, burst into laughter, then helped his friend up off the ground. As the three boys joked amongst themselves, another figure emerged from the forest path and stood in the shadows just beyond the Jack-o-lantern's flickering light. A bitter chill swept through the air, and the midnight tolling of the distant church bell seemed to announce the silent stranger's presence.

The dark figure was tall and completely shrouded by a long black cloak that wavered in the cool autumn breeze. His face was covered by a ghoulish mask that resembled a crudely carved pumpkin. The black sockets of the mask's eyes could not be penetrated by the meager glow of the dim candlelight.

"Who's there?" Greg asked, lowering his voice in an attempt to sound intimidating.

The figure spoke in a deep whisper, "Telling ghost stories during the witching hour on Halloween night? How quaint.

Would you mind if I rested these old bones and shared a tale of my own?"

No one said a word in protest as the figure approached the fire pit and seated himself on a tree stump directly behind the Jack-o-lantern's leering face.

"Some legends say that Jack-o-lanterns can ward off evil spirits," the masked stranger croaked, "while others say that it acts like a beacon for wayward souls, attracting restless ghosts with its glow." He paused to look around him, then said " The native Algonquin tribes named this place the Manitoa Forest. They believed that it was the hunting grounds for an ancient deity named Malsumis, the shadow god who put thorns on trees. There are those who believe these woods are filled with dark spirits that have roamed the earth for centuries."

The boys laughed nervously at his comments and the stranger settled back to begin his tale. "My story took place many years ago, not far from here, in a small town called Parson's Crossing." As he spoke, his raspy voice gave the impression that he had just risen from the grave. "Two boys disappeared on Halloween night in these very woods."

"I've heard that story," Greg interrupted. "Its about that kid, Jonah Trask, who killed his friend and chopped him up with an axe. He supposedly got sent to a mental asylum for the rest of his life."

"That story isn't true," Rob said, smirking and shaking his head. "It's just an urban legend. It didn't really happen."

"Indeed, it did happen," the masked figure replied, "but not the way most people tell it. No one knows the real story—no one, that is, but me." The gravelly throated stranger paused, then asked, "May I continue?"

Rob nodded for him to proceed.

"Their names were Jonah Trask and Todd Garrison. They entered the forest shortly before sundown and lost their sense of direction as night descended. They wandered deeper and deeper into the dense woods until they became hopelessly lost.

"Eventually they heard faint voices in the distance—voices that sounded like someone whispering their names. They followed the sounds to a clearing in the middle of the forest. A ghostly fog shrouded the ground, and moonlight illuminated an old stone well that stood at the center of the hollow.

"The boys slowly crept toward the ancient structure, drawn closer by the hypnotic call from somewhere within. Primitive symbols and carvings of unknown beasts were chiseled into the stones around the well's perimeter. Jonah picked up a loose rock and dropped it into the pit to assess the well's depth, but no sound returned from the darkness below. As the boys peered over the edge of crumbling bricks and down into the gaping maw, a putrid smell of decay rose to meet them.

"The light of the harvest moon glistened upon the wet, mossy stones that led down into the dark recesses of the earth, and as they stared into the depths of the pit, the boys began to discern shapes rising from the shadows. At first they appeared to be no more than tendrils of smoke, reaching upward from the darkness below, but then the mist began to take on more menacing forms. Skeletal arms and writhing black tentacles stretched upward and out of the well, ensnaring the boys in their clutches.

"With a firm hold on both boys, the black limbs began pulling them over the edge and into the well. Todd caught hold of a root with one arm and grabbed his friend with the other, pulling him free from the shadow creatures' grip. Jonah watched in horror as a bony hand dug its black talons into Todd's throat, tearing open his neck, drenching Jonah in a torrent of his friend's blood. Todd's grip relinquished and his body fell limp. Within seconds, he was covered in a mass of constricting tentacles and thorn-like claws that pulled him down into the hellish pit.

"Filled with mortal terror, Jonah fled the grisly scene with all his speed and never looked back."

The masked storyteller paused for a long moment, then

continued his tale. "Two days later, Jonah stumbled out of the woods, covered in Todd Garrison's blood. He told the police his wild story of the old well and the shadow creatures that took his friend, but his unbelievable tale only cast a dark cloud of suspicion upon him.

"The authorities searched the woods, but they never found the well or the boy's body. Nobody believed Jonah Trask's horrific account of what happened and he was locked away in the Northcliff Institution for the Criminally Insane."

"Most people believe that Jonah was insane and that he killed Todd and disposed of his body where no one would ever find it. But in all the years that have passed since that fateful night, Jonah never changed his story.

"Some say that Todd's spirit still roams these woods on Halloween night, searching for his friend who deserted him. They say that he lurks in the darkness and shuns the light and that he will only come near it if he's invited by the living. They warn that if you see him wandering in the dead of night, you should run the other way, or he'll drag you into the dark woods and down into his well where the shadows will feast upon your blood."

"That's some pretty spooky stuff," Greg said, "but I don't believe a word of it."

"No?" the stranger cackled, "but you've heard the tale before. You said so yourselves."

"Yeah," Rob chuckled, "well, that's just a ghost story, and I don't believe in ghosts, or killer shadows, or monsters that prowl the night."

"I see," the storyteller hissed. "Then perhaps you will indulge me with a test of your courage to prove the merit of your words. It's very simple, unless you are afraid of the dark." The masked figure leaned closer and whispered "All you have to do is blow out the candle."

The three boys sat motionless, exchanging timid glances at one another for several moments as the storyteller's words echoed in their heads. Finally Rob leaned in over the top of the Jack-o-lantern and said, “I don’t know who you are mister, but I’m not afraid of you... and I’m not afraid of the dark.”

Before anyone could stop him, Rob took a deep breath and blew out the flickering candle, instantly plunging them into pitch blackness.

When the police found the boy’s blood-spattered campsite the following day, they suspected the worst. The withered husk of a Jack-o-lantern stared at them from the center of the fire pit—its face frozen in a mocking expression of howling laughter. Drag marks on the ground led into the forest, but the trail went cold after a few hundred feet. Search parties scoured the woods for the boy’s bodies, but no traces of any of them was ever found. The news that Jonah Trask had escaped from the Northcliff Institution for the Criminally Insane on Halloween night left the authorities with little hope of ever finding the boys alive.

Tales of dark things prowling the shadows of the Manitoa Forest are still told around campfires, and to this day no one dares to venture into those haunted woods after sundown, especially on Halloween night. Perhaps it is a superstitious fear of the dark itself that keeps them away, or perhaps it is a very real fear of the darkness that lurks within the deepest recesses of the human soul.

# Sanctus Ritus Expulsum Diabolus

III

II

I

VI

IV

V

Vindico Is
Animus Per Illa
Vesica Quod
Iuguolo Bestia
Occultus Intus

# SISTER SALVATION

*by Joseph Vargo and Joseph Iorillo*

Elizabeth roused from a numb state of unconsciousness to find herself caught in a living nightmare. Her vision was the first of her senses to return. She was in a dark chamber, dimly illuminated by candlelight. The rough stone walls suggested a basement or a prison cell. Her body ached from head to foot and she could not move her limbs. Panic seized her as she realized that she was strapped to a cold steel chair that was bolted to the center of the concrete floor. Her wrists were handcuffed to the rusty metal arms of the chair by antique manacles. A leather muzzle was strapped over the lower half of her face, making breathing nearly impossible. Her stunned eyes registered a red circle painted on the floor surrounding her chair, with five large candles set at intervals around the perimeter.

She began gasping and weeping as the sheer horror of her situation became apparent. She was not dreaming. She was horribly awake, and she was going to die here violently.

The last thing she remembered was walking to her car through the parking garage at her accounting firm. She recalled fumbling around in her purse for her car keys but her mind was a blank after that. Her aching head and blurred vision told her that she must have been drugged and abducted. Now she was completely at the mercy of her captor, for what ungodly purpose her mind dared not imagine.

From somewhere in the darkness behind her came the sharp squeal of rusted hinges, alerting her that someone was entering the room. The door slammed shut, followed by the sound of a heavy metal latch being thrown. Elizabeth began trembling and her heart pounded in her chest. She wanted to scream but terror kept her voiceless.

After a long silence, she heard a deep, eerily calm male voice behind her. "The Lord created the earthly realm for his children and bestowed the gift of free will upon them. While the devoted worship the Lord, others falter in their faith, led astray by temptations. But the path we follow must ultimately be one of our own choosing. For Judgment Day shall come, and when we stand before the Lord, we must stand alone."

A long shadow fell across the flickering candles as the man stepped forward and stood before Elizabeth. He wore a black robe with a hood that left his face cloaked in darkness. He spoke again, this time in a whisper that sent a chill through her body. "Fear not, child, for I have come to set you free."

Elizabeth tried to scream but all she could muster was a ragged, hoarse sob. "Why are you doing this to me?" she wailed.

"You were not chosen by random, nor were you chosen by me. The Lord moves in mysterious ways and I am but his humble and ever-faithful servant. My duty is to cleanse your soul of the twisted entity that holds you in its thrall."

The hooded figure turned and stepped deeper into the darkness. There was the rattling of metal upon metal and the squeaking of old wooden casters as he wheeled forth what seemed to be a small, antique surgery table upon which rested several ominous devices and ornate daggers. Elizabeth's trembling dissolved into a wild thrashing as her horrified eyes stared at the gleaming objects that this monster intended to use on her.

"In the thirteenth century," the shadowy figure explained, "the Church began a painful but necessary cleansing of the heresies and abominations that have befallen mankind and forced the children of God off the path of righteousness and into the shadow cast by the Father of Lies. Unclean beliefs, erroneous teachings, witchcraft, and even bodily possession by the fallen angels—all of these crimes were given to us, the Inquisitors, to punish and to cleanse, in order to grant deliverance to the weak souls that had strayed from the light."

He picked up a metal and leather device that resembled a horse's bridle. Tiny, almost imperceptible needle tips protruded from the rusty mouthpiece, and a small winch resided on the front of the mechanism. "This was often referred to as the Confessor. Once it is affixed around your head and the bit is forced in your mouth, a mere turn of the crank will send forth a dozen needles into your gums." He demonstrated by turning the winch, and the tiny steel pinpricks blossomed forth into inch-long spikes.

"Please," she begged, "just let me go. I'll do anything you want."

"Throughout the years certain improvements have been made to heighten the effectiveness of our tools." The hooded figure replaced the bridle on the table and picked up a heavy iron device with four metal rings and levers. An indentation in the shape of a hand was molded into its metal base. "The Mano de Verdad," he said, holding the device up so Elizabeth could see it. "The Hand of Truth. As each lever is thrown, a steel ring is pulled downward into the base, forcing pressure onto the finger, breaking the bone backward against the top knuckle. I assure you, the pain is beyond anything your mind can imagine."

"You're a monster!" Elizabeth shrieked, struggling against her restraints to no avail.

"On the contrary," the hooded figure replied, with something akin to kindness. "I do not relish inflicting pain, but in cases such as yours it is a necessity. I work on behalf of a Godly agent who has been sanctioned by the Church to cleanse human souls of the evil spirits that contaminate them. Her dedication is fierce and unswerving, and her methods may seem cruel, but we have found that pain is the surest way to drive out an invading entity, thus purging the host. Physical torment is often too much for these spirits to bear, for they experience every sensation that your body feels. While you will not perish, the pain will bring you to the brink of death, but only in order to cleanse you of the cowardly spirit that now hides behind your innocent soul."

He stepped toward Elizabeth and slid the base of the iron device beneath her right palm, avoiding any direct contact between her hand and his own. Her manacles made it impossible for her to resist as he clamped her fingers into the steel rings, tightening them just below her fingernails.

"No, please... no!" Elizabeth's voice cracked as she pleaded, but her captor persisted in his work, fastening the Hand of Truth to the chair's arm with a leather strap.

As he finished his work, the man took notice of a silver medallion that hung from a thin chain around Elizabeth's neck. Brushing a finger against the engraved image of a Catholic saint, he studied the familiar icon intently.

"Saint Christopher, the protector," he said, "This evidence of your faith does you credit, my child. Saint Christopher will keep you strong through this ordeal."

Elizabeth desperately tried to reason with the madman. "If I were possessed by a demon, like you say I am, would I be able to wear this—a blessed medallion?"

The inquisitor paused for a moment and turned away, as if contemplating the logic of her argument. Then he said "During my years of service to the Church, I have borne witness to many things that defy earthly explanation. I do not question such matters, for I know full well that the Father of Lies uses such deceits in his unending attempt to divert us from the righteous path. The loathsome beast that lurks inside you has concealed itself well. But fear not, my child, with proper persistence, this unholy entity can be driven out and destroyed." He turned back toward her, resting his fingers on the steel levers of the Hand of Truth and said "Shall we begin?"

"Please don't do this," she begged, "I haven't done anything wrong. I don't deserve to die like this."

"It is neither my desire nor my instruction to kill you," the hooded figure said. He selected a long, ornate dagger from the table, extending his arm until the tip of the blade pressed against her sternum through her blouse. The point drew a solitary drop of blood and Elizabeth cried out. "But, sadly, death does sometimes occur during these sessions because of the weakness of human flesh and the human will. This dagger, however, will bind your blighted spirit to this girl's body, wretched demon." He gestured to a series of other daggers, each of which was engraved with mystic sigils and Latin prayers. "Each of these sacred blades has a specific designation and must be inserted in the proper sequence, penetrating the eyes, the base of the spine and finally the heart. These blessed tools will destroy you, demon, purifying the girl's soul before she expires."

Elizabeth wept and screamed, "There's no demon, you sick bastard! You're going to murder me!"

"Your pleas will do you no good, demon," the man replied tiredly. "I've heard them all before. I know exactly what you are and nothing you say or do can convince me otherwise."

"You've done this before? You're sick," she sobbed. "You're just a sick, twisted psycho who gets off on torturing his victims! Take a look in the mirror. You're the demon!"

"No, my poor child, I am a humble inquisitor, acting on behalf of your eternal soul." He took hold of the lever beside Elizabeth's index finger and, without warning, cranked the handle toward her. The mechanism squealed as the steel ring crushed down upon the bone, breaking her fingertip backward with a sharp crackle.

Elizabeth let loose a sickening wail, completely exhausting the air in her lungs. Undeterred by the girl's shrieks of agony, the inquisitor took hold of the next lever.

"No! No!" she screamed. "Stop! Stop! Stop!"

Ignoring her pleas, the man plunged the handle downward,

cracking the top knuckle of her middle finger against the joint with a force so violent that it caused the fingernail to tear away from the raw flesh.

Elizabeth's screams of agony reached a horrific crescendo of ear-splitting cries.

Taking a step back, the tormentor thrust the dagger in front of him and shouted "Hear me demon, and believe me when I say that I have no misgivings about inflicting unbearable suffering and torment upon your mortal host! I will sacrifice this child, if need be, in order to save her eternal soul!"

The girl's shrieks diminished to gasping sobs. She hung her head and wept, nearly passing out from the excruciating pain.

The inquisitor leaned in close to her, lifting her muzzled chin with his dagger and looked deep into her eyes. "There are six more fingers to go," he said solemnly. "Trust me when I tell you that your thumbs will cause a whole new level of pain. Then we will move on to your toes."

"Kill me," Elizabeth whispered, "please... just kill me." Tears streaked down her cheeks, and a single teardrop fell from her chin, landing on the hand of her tormentor.

The man stiffened, staring down at the droplet on his weathered skin. "No," he whispered. "No." The blessed dagger trembled in his hand, searing the flesh of his palm before it fumbled to the ground, where it spun briefly, its blade gleaming in the candlelight, before coming to rest, the tip pointing accusingly at him.

It was as though he had been jolted by lightning, and every nerve in his body felt as if it were set ablaze. One moment he had been grimly set about his work, thinking of his years of service to Sister Helena—Sister Salvation, as he sometimes thought of her—and the next moment his entire being felt as if it had been bathed in a white-hot fire. It lasted but an instant, and after the initial shock he stood there breathing heavily, a strange calmness pervading his being. There was something wrong inside of him, he could feel it, but his mind seemed unable to protest or investigate the matter further. It was as though a shadow had fallen across his soul and that shadow was now directing his actions. Without being aware of it, he removed the hood that masked his weathered, bearded face. His voice, curiously flat and emotionless, seemed to be coming from far away as he gazed upon the girl in the chair.

"Goodbye, my dear. It's a pity that we didn't have more time together." He moved to the entrance and pulled open the heavy door.

"Don't leave me here," the girl sobbed, "Please!"

Paying no heed to her desperate cries, he slammed the door shut behind him and threw the bolt, abandoning Elizabeth in the dark chamber.

It was now time to report back to Sister Helena. The mere thought of dealing with her made his face twitch with sinister glee. The strange force within him seemed to purr with a ferocious hunger, like a vicious panther sensing the proximity of its prey.

At the cathedral, the vespers service was coming to its conclusion as the sun set, its dying light setting ablaze the stained glass windows in a fury of color. Ignoring the mournful, melodic chanting of the brothers, the man strode across the grounds to the rectory. He descended into the bowels of the church, his boots echoing hollowly on the stone steps.

In Sister Helena's chamber, he saw her silhouetted against the window as she stared out into the churchyard. "You have been gone quite a while," she said softly.

He said nothing.

She turned and studied his face. Her eyebrows raised slightly. "Usually you bow to me in respect, Mr. Ambrose."

He bowed slowly, not taking his eyes off the nun, a slight smile affixed to his thin lips.

"The girl is now freed from her bondage to the dark forces," he said.

"You have served me well throughout the years, Mr. Ambrose. But in this case your work seems to have become... disordered."

The inquisitor's eyes narrowed.

From the pocket of her habit, Sister Helena withdrew the intricately detailed dagger Mr. Ambrose had left near the girl. The sight of the ancient weapon made him slightly recoil as if he were standing too close to a fire.

"You left your tools at the scene," she said. She held the blessed dagger out for him to take.

He could not bring himself to take the hilt of the weapon. His hand trembled and his breathing became ragged.

"Surely you wish to reclaim the sanctified tools of your trade, Mr. Ambrose." She scrutinized his face, her gaze steady and unreadable. "Unless something is preventing you."

Before he could react, she drove the dagger deep into his sternum with one swift plunge. He gasped in surprise, unable to scream. His legs buckled and he fell to his knees.

"This holy dagger has secured the demon within you," Sister Helena said. One by one she removed the other daggers from her robe. "The others shall purify you, Mr. Ambrose, and extinguish the spirit of evil that now holds you in its thrall."

"Our sacred duties have not been easy, but you performed them with exemplary precision. You were the perfect man for the job, Mr. Ambrose. Heartless, and ruthlessly cold—a true relic of the medieval age." She lifted the next dagger high above her head as the inquisitor knelt before her. "I hope you can find solace in the fact that your final sacrifice has set an innocent soul free."

When Mr. Ambrose finally lay on the stone floor with daggers piercing his chest, his eyes, his spine and his heart, Sister Helena again stood by the window, bestowing a kiss of prayer upon the Saint Christopher's medal around her neck, a medal identical to the one her poor, besieged sister wore.

# THE PUMPKIN PATCH

*by Joseph Vargo*

No one had forced Josh or Nick to enter the haunted house alone. They willingly chose to explore its dark and unhallowed corridors, knowing full well of the terrors that lied in wait. The two teens had never been ones to shy away from a challenge and they had earned a reputation as being the local thrillseekers. Although their friends considered them to be fearless, most adults called them reckless and foolhardy. Regardless of opinion, the pair had always found new ways to break the monotony of their adolescent lives, and they had found something special to occupy their interests on Halloween night.

The two friends quietly crept down the dilapidated hallway, examining the forsaken mansion's creepy details. Antique gaslights covered in cobwebs hung at crooked angles and pealing Victorian wallpaper exposed the rotting wallboards beneath. As they walked past a large portrait of an old woman, it changed to reveal a decayed corpse that seemed to offer them a wicked grin.

"You see that?" Nick whispered.

"Shhhh," Josh replied, "there's something around the corner." He motioned to the end of the hallway where a shadow slowly moved across the wall, revealing a large form that awaited them once they turned the corner. "Come on," Josh whispered, as he proceeded to step towards the ominous shadow, "I think it's Old Man Blackwood himself."

Josh let his footsteps fall heavy to announce his approach and Nick, following close behind, did the same. They turned the corner quickly to boldly face the horror that awaited them. A ghoulish old man dressed in a tattered Victorian suit let out a moan as he lunged at them with a large butcher knife. Josh stepped out of the way and tripped his attacker, and as the withered ghoul fell, his knife dropped to the floor. The blade landed point downward and would have imbedded itself into the floorboards, had it actually been made of metal. Instead, the plastic butcher's knife bounced away into the shadows. The fallen ghoul let out a string of obscenities and the teenagers erupted into laughter. Within seconds the haunted house security guards were on top of them.

The exit doors of Blackwood Mansion flew open as the security team threw the teenage punks out before a crowd of onlookers.

"You can't touch me!" Josh yelled, "I'm only seventeen. I'll sue your ass!" The two began walking toward the parking lot when the actor portraying Old Man Blackwood emerged from the exit, adjusting his scraggly gray wig.

Nick reached beneath his leather jacket and yelled, "Hey old man... lose something?" He withdrew his hand, which now held the plastic butcher knife and brandished the prop high for the crowd to see. The people in line erupted into cheers and laughter, and the two darted for the parking lot with the security guards in hot pursuit. The older guards were soon out of breath and gave up the chase after a few hundred yards.

As the two pranksters sat on the hood of Nick's '72 Firebird, they laughed and popped open a couple of beers. "We're legends now," Josh said, hitting the top of his Rolling Rock against Nick's bottle.

"Bravo," said a voice from behind them. The two turned to see a petite girl, clad in full goth attire, clapping her hands as she approached them. "That was pretty funny," she said as she sauntered to a halt in front of them, "and I'll admit it took some stones to pull it off, but it was far from legendary."

"Oh well," Nick replied with a grin, "two out of three ain't bad."

The girl returned his smile, with a perfect set of pearly whites, framed by black lipstick. Her skin was pale, in contrast to her jet black hair, which matched every stitch of her wardrobe.

"I'm Josh, that's Nick. And you are?"

Nick interrupted before she could utter a response,"Wait, let me guess, Raven? No...Lily..."

"Elvira! That's it," Josh said, pointing his finger at the pentagram pendant that clung to her chest.

"Whatever," the girl replied with a smirk, "I just thought that you guys might be up for something more challenging tonight."

"I'm always up for anything," Josh said with a wink.

Ignoring his crude flirtation, Elvira asked "Have either of you ever heard of Sally Withers?"

Nick was the first to chime in."You mean Crazy Sally, the old witch who lives by herself on the farm way back in Kelsie's Woods? I hear she catches stray dogs and cats and grinds them into fertilizer for her garden. She's supposedly got this huge pumpkin patch."

Not to be outdone by Nick's knowledge of local folklore, Josh added "I heard she performs these Satanic rituals at midnight where she dances and chants weird incantations to make her pumpkins grow."

A devilish grin appeared on Elvira's face. "If you guys want to raise some real hell on Halloween, you should cruise out to her farm, sneak into her garden, and steal the biggest pumpkin you can carry."

"And then what?" Josh asked, shrugging his shoulders.

"I don't know, bring it back here, carve your names in it, douse it with lighter fluid and push it down Cemetery Hill. It doesn't matter what you do with it, it's just the fact that we stole a pumpkin from a witch on Halloween night."

"We?" Nick asked.

"Hey," Elvira replied, "it was my idea."

The two thrillseekers looked at each other and smiled, silently acknowledging that the pumpkin patch caper sounded like fun.

"Let's roll," Nick said, climbing into the driver's seat of the Firebird. As he turned the ignition key and revved the engine, Elvira opened the passenger door and slid in beside him, followed by Josh who squeezed in next to her in the front seat. The trio left the parking lot in a cloud of dust and flying gravel and headed west down the Old Valley Road.

"Wanna beer?" Josh asked, offering her a Rolling Rock.

"Thanks, but one of us should keep a clear head. I don't want to end up on the wrong side of a witch's spell."

Josh smirked. "It's like I always say, live fast, die young..." he paused to take a final swig from his beer, "and leave a good-lookin' corpse." As if to add dramatic emphasis to his statement, Josh flicked the empty bottle out the window and it crashed onto the road behind them.

"Hey!" Nick yelled, "we gotta drive back this way."

"Just stay on the right side of the road then," Josh retorted with a laugh.

"That's only if we make it out of there alive," Elvira added with a devilish laugh of her own.

As they drove along the asphalt road that led to Kelsie's Woods, they were gradually engulfed by a thick fog that had claimed the entire valley basin. "Slow down or you'll pass it," Elvira said, pointing to an overgrown path to the left side of the road.

Nick screeched to a halt then pulled off the blacktop and onto the dirt drive that snaked back into the woods. A rusted mailbox with the name "WITHERS" was attached to a post right beside a sign that said "NO TRESPASSERS."

Josh smiled and said "Let's go find the great pumpkin."

The three stayed within the shadows of the treeline as they ventured deeper onto the property. After several hundred yards, they could see the pumpkin patch beside an old farmhouse.

"No lights," Nick whispered, "it doesn't look like anyone's home."

"Of course not," Josh replied, "it's Halloween. Ole' Sally's probably out flying around on her broomstick tonight."

The three left the cover of trees and crept through the open field as silently as possible. The fog seemed to grow more dense with each step they took. By the time the teens reached the pumpkin patch, they could barely see one another. A cold breeze swept past them emitting a ghostly moan. A rustling sound from somewhere ahead alerted them to another presence in the mist.

The fog relented for a moment to reveal a tall figure dressed in tattered clothes towering over Elvira. The silent wraith loomed before the girl with its arms outstretched, as if to capture her in its diabolical grasp.

"Look out!" Nick shouted as he leapt to her aid, diving on top of her. The two hit the dirt, landing amidst the pumpkins that covered the ground.

Within seconds Josh had found his way through the fog to stand between his fallen friends and the ominous figure. He quickly assessed the situation, then began to laugh out loud, saying, "Way to go hero. It's just a freakin' scarecrow."

Josh stared at the creepy-looking straw man that had been tied to a tall wooden post, his eyes following the crude stitchwork that held the scarecrow's burlap face together.

"Hey," Nick whispered as he and Elvira picked themselves up off the ground, "these pumpkins ain't so big. They're all normal sized."

"Forget about the pumpkins," Josh said, his eyes still transfixed upon the straw man, "we're takin' Mr. Stitch here."

Josh reached out to grab hold of the scarecrow's raggedy coat, but before his fingers could touch it, he felt something tugging at his ankle. "What the hell..." Looking down, he could see that a pumpkin vine had ensnared his foot, and as he struggled to free himself, another snake-like tendril reached upward and wrapped itself around his other ankle. "Nick... help! The vines... they're alive."

Nick took a step toward his friend and was immediately set upon by the network of vines that surrounded him. They reached up in serpentine fashion, wrapping themselves around his torso and pulling him down to the ground. Before they could wriggle free, both teens were completely entangled in the vines.

Unable to move, they watched in horror as one by one, the pumpkins began to rise up and undergo a sinister transformation into monstrous forms. Black eyes opened from narrow slits and mouths gaped wide to reveal jagged fangs. As they rose, skeletal bodies emerged from the ground beneath them. Their orangish-brown flesh crackled and popped as the things stretched their limbs, and long, bony fingers extended from their wrinkled arms.

The goblin army soon surrounded them. The thick vines had constricted tight around their chests and throats, making it difficult to breathe and impossible to scream. Elvira stood as silent and still as she could amidst the creatures, as if afraid to draw their attention, then she erupted into wicked laughter.

As she stepped toward her entangled friends, the vines parted before her. She knelt between her two comrades and spoke in a calm voice. "Dogs and cats make good fertilizer for my pets, but once they've sprouted, their appetites become much more... demanding."

Josh and Nick writhed in terror as the creatures drew closer and descended upon them, yet the harder they struggled, the tighter the vines became.

"I'm sorry we weren't properly introduced," the girl continued, "My name's Sally. You boys are trespassing on my property, and there's a high price to be paid for that." She wiped her finger across a trickle of blood that seeped from where the course vine had dug into Nick's flesh then held it to her lips and licked it, saying "Mmmm... how sweet."

Sally rose to her feet and resumed her speech. “Human blood is a precious ingredient to many spells from the black books. It can keep a person young forever, especially when it’s untainted. Even better when it comes from those who willingly enter unhallowed ground. As you said, live fast, die young...” She stopped and flashed them a sinister grin, her mouth now filled with jagged fangs. “Unfortunately, I’m afraid that neither of you will leave a very good looking corpse once my pets and I are done with you, but you’re hardly in a position to protest. And after all, as you said yourself... two out of three ain’t bad.”

# THE WESTGATE PHANTOM

*by Joseph Vargo*

They say evil exists in the hearts of men. They say that monsters are merely products of superstition—figments of overactive imaginations. But I know the truth. I've seen things that shouldn't be—spirits of people who died long ago and nightmarish creatures from the blackest depths of Hell. I've stared Death itself in the face, and I've learned a lot about the origins of evil. Trust me, you don't want to know the truth.

My name is Robert Morgan. I'm a reporter and paranormal investigator. I've seen my share of hoaxes in my time, and it's led me to develop a somewhat cynical attitude toward most cases of alleged supernatural activity. But the way I see it, you've got to be skeptical if you intend to dig up the truth. And that's exactly what I dug up at the old Westgate Hotel.

Built in 1886, the Westgate was the epitome of Victorian elegance. Its registry boasted only the wealthiest and most prestigious clientele from America and Europe. Nestled in the foothills of the Adirondacks, the hotel was constructed on a natural plateau overlooking the dense forests of the Manitoa Valley. During the Great Depression, the old hotel was purchased by a wealthy doctor named Miles Wincott who converted the sprawling estate into a hospital and sanitarium. That's when the Westgate's haunted history began.

In the 1930s, the hospital staff started reporting numerous

incidents of strange sounds and shadowy forms in the various rooms and hallways of the hospital. These unexplainable occurrences were followed by a string of disappearances. Patients and staff alike went missing. Investigators chalked up the mounting unsolved cases to stress brought on by strained working conditions in a depressing environment. But the most mysterious disappearance of all was that of Dr. Wincott himself. On the evening of April 30th, 1942, the good doctor finished his nightly rounds, retired to his office and was never seen again. To add to the weirdness, the police investigation shows that his office door was bolted from the inside and there were no other visible means of exiting the room.

One year after Dr. Wincott's disappearance, the deed to the land reverted to the state and the Westgate was purchased by new owners who commenced to convert the old building back into a hotel. The renovations and restorations were completed within two years and the Westgate opened its doors as a luxury resort once more in 1944.

There hadn't been any reports of paranormal activity for nearly thirty years, until a recent development left its deadly mark on the place. One of the guests, a young woman by the name of Theresa Frasier, was found dead in her bed with a look of sheer terror frozen on her face. The police investigators found no signs of foul play. The coroner ruled that she had died of a massive coronary due to internal trauma, but there were no visible injuries on any other parts of her body. When I spoke to the medical examiner he told me that he had never seen anything like it, confiding to me that it was as if her heart had been crushed from the inside.

I had always wanted to investigate the Westgate to see if something unnatural really did wander its halls in the dead of night, but I had a long list of other alleged hauntings that my editor wanted me to look into first. Theresa Frasier's mysterious death moved the old hotel to the top of my list.

I checked into the hotel on March 15th, ten days after the

grisly incident, and requested to stay in the same room in which the young woman had died—suite 312. The old man behind the hotel desk squinted and looked me up and down before reluctantly handing me the key to the room. As I signed the registry, he scrutinized my signature, as if looking for some tell-tale sign in my handwriting that would allow him to interpret my true intentions for staying in that particular suite. His suspicions apparently satisfied, the strange old man gave me a wry grin, then snapped his fingers to summon a bellhop.

A lanky young man appeared at my side and picked up my suitcase, saying "Right this way, sir." Then, without another word, he led me across the lobby and escorted me into the elevator.

As soon as the antique elevator doors closed, the bellhop began speaking in a hushed tone. "You're a reporter, aren't you? I can always tell when someone's here to investigate the hauntings."

"What makes you think that the hotel is haunted?" I asked.

"I'm the resident expert on ghosts. My name's Danny. I've always been interested in this kind of thing, you know, the occult and paranormal stuff. Trust me, this place is as haunted as they come."

The elevator lurched to a halt as it reached the third floor and as the doors slid open, Danny stopped talking.

As we exited the elevator, I asked "So what's the deal with the creepy old guy behind the front desk?"

"Oh, that's just Mr. Collins, the hotel manager. He's a little eccentric, but he's harmless. Now her," he motioned his head slightly toward a large matronly woman who was pushing a maid's cart down the hallway, "she's a different story. That's Hilda, head of housekeeping. We call her Broomhilda, you know, like the witch." Danny brandished a smile and a nod as he passed the woman in the hallway and she returned his greeting with a scowl of contempt.

We proceeded to the end of the hall and stopped before the door to 312. I gave Danny a ten-dollar tip and with a wink told him to keep me posted about anything unusual in the hotel.

Inside my room, I opened the case file and examined the coroner's report. A police photo showed the exact position in which Theresa Frasier's body was found. Her arms were straight out to her sides and her hands hung beyond the edges of the bed. It seemed as if her body had been laid out in some sort of ritualistic pose. There were no ligature marks on her wrists and no apparent signs of a struggle in the room, suggesting that she met her death without resistance.

After I unpacked, I spent the next few hours referencing the case file and adding some notes to my laptop journal. Around 9 p.m., I headed down to the hotel restaurant for a late dinner. I had intended to dine alone, but I saw Danny peeking out from behind a column near the kitchen several times while I ate. I waited till I was done with my meal then waved him over to join me at my table.

"What's on your mind, kid?"

Danny's eyes shifted from side to side, as if to check that no one was eavesdropping on our conversation, then he began speaking in a low tone. "You asked me to let you know about anything unusual around the hotel."

"What do you know?"

"Well... no one's supposed to talk about it, and I could get in trouble for telling you, but there have been some other strange incidents over the past few months."

"Like what?"

"Some of the guests have reported seeing a man dressed in an old-fashioned suit standing in their rooms at night. We call him the phantom. They say he doesn't say or do anything. He just stands there watching them in the darkness. One of the people who saw him claimed that he walked right through a solid wall."

"Interesting."

"There's more. Have you heard the stories about the doctor who ran the Westgate when it used to be a sanitarium?"

"Dr. Wincott?"

Danny nodded as he slid an old black and white photograph across the table to me, then leaned in close to whisper, "Well, I showed this photo to one of the guests who reported seeing the phantom in her room and she swore that it was the same man." The aged photo showed a slim man in a top hat and Victorian overcoat posed in front of the doors to the hotel.

"That's Miles Wincott, back in 1927," Danny said.

As I stared at the piercing eyes of the man in the photo I was overcome with a strange feeling—there was something very familiar about his face.

"Do you really believe in ghosts, Mr. Morgan?"

"I never used to," I replied, downing a shot of whiskey, "but I've witnessed some things that have dwindled my skepticism." Reaching a finger beneath my collar, I pulled out the raven's claw pendant that I wore around my neck. "Now you could call me cautiously superstitious."

"What's that?" Danny asked, eyeing the talisman with reverent curiosity.

"Oh, just a little something that saved me from a grisly demise at the hands of a voodoo witch," I said with a wink. While the kid's eyes remained transfixed on the black talon, I asked, "Do you have access to the basement, Danny?"

"Why?"

"What would you say to accompanying me on a little excursion after hours?"

"You mean like a ghost hunt?"

"Yeah, something like that."

Danny's eyes widened. "I could get the master key ring from the manager's office."

"Great. I'll meet you in the lobby at midnight. Bring a flashlight, and don't tell anyone else."

Danny nodded and left the table without another word.

After dinner I explored the hotel museum in an annex off of the main lobby. As I scanned the walls lined with framed letters and photos of famous people who had stayed there, I noticed something odd. There wasn't a single photo of Dr. Wincott on display. A preserved blueprint from 1937 showed the floor plans of the Westgate when it was a sanitarium. Dr. Wincott's office was located in the lower level of the south wing. Interestingly, it appeared that the south wing was never fully renovated when the asylum was converted back into a hotel.

As I studied the antique blueprint, a voice from behind me startled me. "The Westgate has quite a colorful history, wouldn't you agree?"

I turned quickly to see Mr. Collins, the front desk manager standing behind me in the gallery. "Yes," I responded, "very colorful indeed, but I'm curious as to why there aren't any photos of Miles Wincott on display."

Mr. Collins' eyes narrowed behind his thick glasses. "There are some things that are best left in the past." The old man stepped back into the shadows of the gallery and said, "I do hope you enjoy your stay with us, Mr. Morgan," then he turned and walked out of the room.

A slight shudder ran down my spine. I don't care what the kid said about 'harmless' old Mr. Collins, the guy gave me the willies.

It was around 11 p.m. when I finally retired to my room to get a little rest before the big ghost hunt. I set a blessed gris-gris candle on my nightstand and opened a box of matches and stuck one between my teeth like a toothpick then lay on top of the covers of my bed. I stretched my arms out wide, assuming the position of Theresa Frasier's body, and laid there contemplating the few clues I had uncovered.

After staring at the ceiling for several minutes, I began to think my eyes were playing tricks on me. At first, I began to see a thin layer of green smoke spreading across the ceiling, then the smoke began to slowly creep down the walls and take on sinewy forms that swayed in serpentine fashion. The effect was mesmerizing, and I could feel my body growing numb. I tried to sit up, but I was unable to move. I watched as the ghostly tendrils crept across the floor and up onto the bed beside me. The hypnotic green mist slowly grew darker, forming a large black shadow that blotted out the entire ceiling as I lay paralyzed and completely helpless beneath it. The jet-black form looked like an enormous spider looming over me, encasing me within its writhing legs.

My will to resist began to fade, and I could feel myself growing dizzy and on the verge of losing consciousness. I forced my eyes closed and reached for the matchstick that was clenched between my teeth. As long as my eyes were shut, I seemed to regain some control over my body, although even the slightest movement required all of my concentration. I inched my hand toward my face and grabbed the matchstick then stretched my arm toward the candle on the nightstand. I struck the match on the rough edge of the table and heard the sound of the flame igniting. I needed to see the candle in order to light it, but I dared not open my eyes for more than a split second, for fear of losing my will to the hypnotic monstrosity above me.

And now I felt a new sensation that filled my pounding heart with terror. Something had grabbed hold of my wrist, latching onto my arm with crushing strength, preventing me from reaching the blessed candle. It felt like the icy grip of death itself. I could feel the air around my face growing colder, betraying the horrifying fact that whatever had hold of my wrist was now leaning in close to me. And then a voice echoed inside my head like an irresistible command that was impossible to ignore.

"Open your eyes," the deep voice whispered.

I no longer possessed the will to resist. I had to obey the voice. I opened my eyes to see a skeletal man wearing a top hat and old suit leaning over my bed. His eyes were solid black and his lips were drawn back to reveal long, jagged fangs, like those of a crocodile. Although I only gazed upon the grisly visage for a brief second, I recognized its face. It was the face of Dr. Miles Wincott.

Just then, the flame of the burning matchstick touched my

fingers, and though my natural instincts demanded that I drop the match, my instinct for survival made me hold on tight. The sensation of pain momentarily restored my willpower and I thrust my arm toward the candle, straining with all my might against the living nightmare that held me in its clutches. As soon as the match met with the candle's wick, the monstrous doctor relinquished his grip and faded from sight. With an unearthly shriek, the mist retreated back up to the ceiling and completely dissipated.

I sprang up from my bed and quickly surveyed he room. There was no one there, but the gris-gris candle cast an eerie glow from the nightstand, verifying the fact that what I had just experienced was not a nightmare or figment of my imagination.

I hurriedly got dressed and grabbed my pocket flashlight, my camera phone, a box of matches and a candle, and set out to meet Danny. He was already waiting for me in the lobby, peering around nervously like a jailhouse snitch. When he saw me, he smiled like a kid on Christmas morning, followed by a look of grave concern. I must've appeared a little disheveled after my close encounter with the Westgate Phantom.

"You okay?" Danny asked. "You don't look so good."

"I'm fine," I said, wiping the sweat from my face. "Let's get going."

Danny turned and quickly led the way. I followed him through the servant's entrance and down a back staircase that twisted deep into the subterranean realms far below the old hotel. At the bottom of the stairs, we found ourselves in a large room that held several boilers and furnaces. Half a dozen corridors led out of the room, heading in various directions.

"Which way leads to the south wing?" I asked.

Without hesitation, Danny pointed his flashlight down a narrow corridor and answered, "That way. Why?"

"I saw an old floor plan of this place and it looks like there's a good-sized area down there that never got renovated. I think they just sealed it off, and according to the blueprint, it used to be Doc

Wincott's mortuary."

Danny's eyes grew wide. "You mean like a morgue, for dead bodies? Right here, beneath the hotel?"

"Can you think of a better place to search for ghosts?"

Danny smiled and said, "This is so cool."

We proceeded along the passageway for a few hundred feet. After several turns, the narrow corridor came to a dead end at a brick wall that was partially covered by an old tarp. I lifted the tarp to discover a hole in the brick wall, roughly four feet high. Several broken bricks lay alongside a large sledgehammer just inside the opening.

"Someone busted through the wall," Danny whispered.

"It sure looks that way, Danny boy. Come on, let's have a look inside." I ducked beneath the jagged bricks and stepped inside the opening, then picked up the sledgehammer and slung it over my shoulder.

"Shouldn't we leave that here, you know, so the cops can dust it for prints or something?" Danny asked.

"Right now I'm more worried about whoever might have left their fingerprints on this thing, and making sure they don't sneak up behind me and clean my clock with it."

Danny nodded in agreement, saying, "Point well-taken."

The sealed chamber opened into a brick hallway about forty feet long with four doorways along each wall. A thick layer of dust and cobwebs covered everything and a musty smell permeated the stale air. The first room we entered held two medical examination tables, fitted with leather restraining straps. A rusted machine that looked like an antique drill press loomed above the head of one table, while a large iron vise rested at the foot of the other.

The next room down held more sinister-looking devices with blades, spikes, levers and cranks. The back wall of the room was covered with oak paneling and as I approached it, I could see that the dust on the floor had been disturbed, forming a path right up to the wooden wall. I knocked on the paneling and a hollow echo resonated from the wall.

"There's a secret entrance here."

I surveyed the wall with my flashlight beam, but couldn't find any apparent way to open the door.

"Maybe one of these levers will open it," Danny said as he reached toward the controls to a large device with rusted gears and a long scythe-like blade.

"Don't touch anything!" I barked, startling Danny, causing him to jump. "Sorry, kid. I just don't want to get my head sliced off by any of these crazy machines." Danny smiled nervously and slowly stepped away from the ominous device.

Upon closer inspection, I noticed that all but one of the levers on the control panel were covered with cobwebs. Using the head of the sledgehammer like a hook, I kept my distance and grabbed hold of the curious lever and yanked it down. With the squeal of metal grinding on metal, the central portion of the oak-paneled wall slid open, revealing a stone staircase leading further into the black depths of the abyss.

"This is awesome," Danny said, with a hint of nervous trepidation in his voice.

I led the way and the kid followed close behind. We descended the narrow stairs to arrive in a large stone chamber deep below the hotel's basement. The stagnant air was deathly cold and carried the pungent smell of mildew. The masonry of the walls was reminiscent of the stonework in a medieval castle. Three arched doorways were set into the surrounding walls and Victorian-style gaslights hung above each of the entrances. The door to our right was closed, as was the one at the far end of the hall, but the doorway on our left was wide open.

Danny looked completely awestruck. "What the hell is this place?" The air was cold enough to see his breath as he spoke.

"I think we found old Doc Wincott's secret lair."

We cautiously made our way to the open door and entered the room to discover a vast array of medical horrors inside. Cabinets and bookcases filled the chamber, displaying antique restraining devices, saws, drills, and skulls with holes in them. As I stepped further into the room, Danny stood frozen in the doorway, surrounded by the shadowy silhouettes of ungodly mutations that seemed to reach out from every dark corner. Slowly, the kid proceeded to follow me further into the chamber of horrors.

"Maybe we should start heading back," Danny said, his voice reflecting his growing concern, "I mean, no one knows we're down here, and it might not be a good idea to..."

"Shhhh," I cut him off abruptly in mid-sentence.

Danny stopped in his tracks, and as the room fell silent, a sound echoed from somewhere behind us.

"I don't think we're alone down here," I whispered.

"Maybe it's just a rat."

"Maybe... maybe not. Just be careful."

As my flashlight scanned the cobwebbed chamber, my eyes began to focus clearly on the horrors within. The brick walls were covered with crude diagrams of bizarre surgical procedures and yellowed photographs of experiments gone horribly wrong. A row of bottles held human teeth, finger bones and various large insects. The gaping eyes of pale abominations peered out from tall jars of formaldehyde, and the tops of the shelves were lined with the twisted skeletal remains of monstrous freaks of nature. On a central shelf amidst the doctor's various keepsakes there sat a small antique frame. As I directed my flashlight onto the dusty memento, I could see that the picture was missing, and a disturbing realization began to sink in.

"Danny," I asked "where'd you get that old photo of Miles Wincott?" But Danny didn't reply. I shone my flashlight beam behind me, but there was no one there. With a firm grip on the sledgehammer, I stepped back into the hall, shining my flashlight in every direction, but the kid was nowhere to be found. He had simply vanished into thin air.

"Danny?" I whispered, "Danny?"

Just then, as if in response to my call, I began to hear faint noises that sounded like a cross between the insane giggling of a child and the desperate whimpering of a wounded animal. I directed my flashlight across the hallway, and the door which had been completely closed a few moments ago now stood partially open. As I silently crept across the hall, it became apparent that the strange sounds were coming from somewhere inside the chamber before me. I pushed the door fully open with the head of the sledgehammer and cautiously entered the room.

Several rows of wooden morgue drawers lined the far wall of the chamber. One of the upper drawers was half-open and a dark liquid was dripping from it, forming a thick pool on the dusty floor below. My grip tensed around the handle of the sledgehammer as I stepped across the room. As I neared the open body drawer, I felt a sharp pain in the back of my neck. I whirled around to see the silhouette of a lanky figure standing in the doorway holding a large syringe. And then I blacked-out.

When I came to, I found myself unable to move, lying on a cold, hard surface in a dimly lit room. My ankles and wrists were strapped to a steel operating table and a leather harness had been tightly secured around my chin and forehead, preventing me from moving my head. I shifted my gaze around the chamber to see several shelves filled with old occult books. Dozens of candles among the bookshelves cast strange shadows throughout the room. A row of human skulls stared at me from an antique cabinet to my right. A large inverted triangle, nearly six feet in diameter, was painted on the brick wall in front of me, surrounded by a circle of unknown writing, similar to Celtic runes. A lone figure stood in the shadows at the far end of the room.

"Welcome to the inner sanctum of the Westgate, Mr. Morgan." A sickening feeling swept over me as I realized who the voice belonged to. Danny stepped forward into the candlelight. He was wearing a white doctor's frock and holding a tattered old book in his hands. "Did you know that according to Sumerian mythology, the West Gate of Mesopotamia was said to be a physical portal that led to the underworld?"

"That's a fascinating bit of trivia, Danny. You should write a book on the subject."

"Don't condescend to me, Mr. Morgan. You're really in no position to make me angry." Danny snapped his book shut and set it down on a steel table that held scalpels, bone saws and other surgical tools. "I know what you're thinking. You think I'm insane, but I can assure you that my mind has never been more focused."

"Focused? On what?" I asked.

"As I told you when we first met, I've held a lifelong interest in the occult and supernatural. That's why I took the job at the Westgate. I discovered the old blueprint in the hotel museum, just as you did, and realized that there was an area beneath the south wing that had been sealed-off for some mysterious reason. I was overwhelmed with curiosity as to what dark treasures might have been buried beneath the old sanitarium. Once I broke through into the sealed hall, I uncovered Dr. Wincott's play area, including his personal library and ritual chamber. After studying his research, I was fascinated by what he had discovered and have since dedicated my life to continuing his work."

"And what work might that be?"

"It's actually quite remarkable—in a macabre sort of way. You see, the doctor ran his sanitarium to house and treat patients who were suffering from paranoid delusions—poor lost souls who were tormented by vivid nightmares and plagued by visions of hellish creatures. Many people believed that Dr. Wincott could ease their pain, but after reading his journals I discovered his sinister secret. You'll notice that some of these journals are quite old. They date back over four hundred years. But the truly astounding thing is that all of the entries are written in the same handwriting."

"So what are you saying? That the doctor was a four-hundred year-old sorcerer who found a way to cheat death?"

"That's exactly what I'm saying, Mr. Morgan. You see, the

doctor performed black masses and ancient rituals to summon forth demonic creatures from the shadows to do his bidding. These living nightmares drove his victims mad, turning them into raving lunatics who seemed to suffer from psychotic delusions. The good doctor had them committed to his care, then lobotomized them and claimed their money and their possessions."

"So what happened to him? If he found a way to live forever, where is he now?"

"That's a good question. He seems to have vanished. His journals end abruptly. Maybe he found a way to transcend his physical state. Maybe he's still here with us, in this hotel, but on a completely different plane of existence."

"Maybe he was devoured by his own demons," I added.

"Ah, the eternal pessimist, Mr. Morgan. You know, there was a time, not so long ago, when doctors implemented medical procedures to correct negative attitudes, such as yours."

Danny turned to the table of surgical instruments and picked up a long steel spike that looked like a ten-inch needle. "I found some of the doctor's old instruments—tools of the trade, so to speak. They're quite crude by today's standards, but still quite effective."

Danny held the surgical spike a few inches from his own face to examine it closely. "This was used for early lobotomy techniques. The spike was inserted beneath the eyeball and driven through the back of each eye socket, puncturing the skull and destroying the frontal lobes of the brain."

Danny stepped toward me and placed the needle at the corner of my left eye, and as he did, I began to notice a faint green mist creeping across the ceiling above him. Raising a small steel hammer directly over the spike, Danny said "Pleasant dreams, Mr. Morgan." But before he could land the blow, a black tendril emerged from the unearthly mist, wrapping itself around his wrist like an enormous python. Danny tried to break free from the constricting grip, but as he struggled two more serpentine tendrils dropped down from the mist above him, entwining his torso in oily black bonds. He strained against the squirming tendrils that held him captive as a gigantic spidery mass of writhing shadows slowly descended from the mist.

Across the room, the inverted triangle painted on the wall began to glow with an eerie green light, then the bricks inside the design faded away, revealing a portal to an unknown dimension of living nightmares. A cloud of black smoke churned just inside the opening and a dark form emerged through the curtain of writhing shadows. At first, the figure appeared to be no more than a vague silhouette of a man wearing a top hat and cape, but as it stepped further into the room, its ghastly features were illuminated by the eerie green glow. Dead eyes squinted from the skeletal face of the cadaverous creature that had once been Dr. Miles Wincott. As the ghoulish doctor stepped toward his captive prey, the serpentine tendrils relinquished their grip and Danny stood frozen in place beneath the phantom's diabolical thrall.

The skeletal fiend leaned in close to Danny and hissed, "First the right eye." A look of terror swept across Danny's face as he slowly raised the surgical spike and turned the point toward himself, holding it directly in front of his own right eyeball. His hand trembled for a moment as he seemed to be fighting the doctor's hypnotic command, then with one swift jab, he plunged the spike deep into his own right eye socket.

As the blood oozed down Danny's cheek, the doctor whispered, "Now the next." Danny slowly withdrew the ten-inch needle from his eye socket then held it before his own face once more. This time there was no hesitation and Danny's arm violently jerked forward as he shoved the needle far into his left eye, driving the spike up into his own brain. Danny's legs buckled beneath him and he dropped to the floor in a whimpering heap.

Picking up a scalpel from the instrument table, the ghoulish phantom then turned to me. His black eyes glistened in the candlelight as he leaned in over me, extending the gleaming blade toward my face. I struggled in vain to turn away, straining my neck muscles against the leather harness that secured my head to the steel table. The unholy abomination seemed to revel in my torment and began to cackle wickedly as he waved the scalpel through the air, bringing it closer and closer to my throat.

Suddenly, the sadistic fiend stopped and I could see that his lifeless eyes had locked upon the raven talisman around my neck. He slowly reached toward the ebony talon, touching it and lifting it with one bony finger. Then the ghoulish doctor smiled at me with his hideous crocodile fangs and lowered the scalpel to my chest. I barely felt a thing as the razor-sharp blade sliced through my skin, but the warm trickle of blood betrayed the fact that one or more incisions had been made. The doctor then cut through the leather strap that bound my left arm to the operating table, and with a tip of his top hat he turned and stepped back through the portal in the wall.

The green glow of the ritual circle began to fade and the opening in the bricks started to grow smaller, but before it closed completely, a black tendril emerged from the darkness within and slithered across the floor to wrap itself around Danny's ankles. Danny clawed at the cobblestones as the serpentine appendage dragged him toward the shrinking portal and the ravenous storm of shadows that raged within. With a sickening, whimpering cry, he was swallowed by the churning blackness as the portal collapsed inward, sealing the hellish gateway, and then the room fell deathly silent.

I quickly freed myself from the remaining restraints and searched the chamber, but found no trace of Danny. I examined the ritual circle and searched the bricks for an opening, but the wall was solid. I took some photos of the inverted triangle and surrounding scrawlings, right before I demolished the wall with my sledge hammer. I packed up the doctor's journals in a box and set fire to them in the woods behind the hotel. I stood guard and watched them burn to a pile of cinders. I wasn't going to take any chances on Dr. Wincott's research falling into the wrong hands again. Like creepy old Mr. Collins said, some things are best left in the past.

Unfortunately, without any evidence, no one was likely to believe my story, but that didn't stop me from submitting it for the discerning scrutiny of my loyal readers. As for the raven talisman, I don't know whether to destroy this thing or never take it off. It's either going to save my neck from the Devil or send my soul to Hell.

On a final note, the incisions the doctor made on my chest have finally healed. The scars form a strange arcane symbol, just over my heart. I have no doubt that this unknown marking will lead me to further dark mysteries which I will be compelled to investigate. Somehow I get the sickening feeling that I haven't seen the last of the diabolical Dr. Wincott, but as far as I'm concerned, the case of the Westgate Phantom is closed.

# THE DOLL

*by Joseph Vargo*

It sat on the top shelf of the bookcase in my room amidst a menagerie of other neglected toys—the evil little harlequin doll. Its porcelain face was crackled and painted with garish clown make-up, framed by twisted strands of black and white hair. Its mouth was frozen in a maniacal smile, and its eyes followed you wherever you moved in the room. The doll's clothes were a patchwork of blue and scarlet satin, adorned with tiny bells for buttons. I was afraid to go anywhere near it, and when I laid in bed at night, the doll stared at me from across the room, its unblinking eyes glistening in the darkness.

When I asked my older brother to get rid of the doll, he refused, and said that the thing scared him too. Then he told me the real story about where the sinister toy came from. He said that the doll used to belong to Mr. Matheson, an old man who lived down the street who passed away in his sleep one night. My brother said that Mr. Matheson didn't just die in his sleep. He said the doll killed him. He told me that the doll came alive one night and slit the old man's throat with his straight razor. Then he said the clown sliced out his heart and ate it. He said that's how the doll stayed alive. I pretended not to be afraid and told him that his stories didn't bother me, but every night I went to sleep with the covers pulled over my head and prayed to God that I'd be safe.

After several months of restless nights, my parents went away and left us alone for the evening, leaving my brother in charge. They made us both promise to behave while they were gone, and of course we lied and swore we would. My brother didn't say a word to me all night, until it was time for me to go to sleep. Before he closed the door to my room, he whispered to me that it was the anniversary of the night that Mr. Matheson died, and that the doll would be hungry tonight.

As I laid in bed that night, I heard the low rumbling of thunder, announcing the approach of a distant storm. Soon, jagged streaks of lightning tore through the night sky, accompanied by ear-splitting thunderstrikes. As the storm grew, rain pounded against my window and lightning lit up my room at irregular intervals. I buried my head beneath my blankets and occasionally opened the covers enough to peak out from below. Lightning flashed sporadically to illuminate the toy shelf. The clown looked even more menacing in the flickering glow. As each flash lit up his face, he glared at me with his evil grimace then disappeared into the shadows as the room returned to darkness. One immense burst of lightning revealed something different about the doll. The strobing light caught the glint of something shiny clutched tightly in his porcelain hands—something long and metallic, that looked like one of my mother's crochet needles.

I pulled the covers closed and began to whisper a prayer, but was interrupted by a crashing sound, as if something had fallen to the floor. My heart pounded and my breath grew heavy as I peered out from beneath my covers. Another flash of lightning streaked through the room and I saw that the clown was no longer sitting on the shelf. Then I heard a scratching noise that sounded as if something were scurrying across my bedroom floor. I tried to cry out, but my throat had gone completely dry. *This wasn't happening,* I thought. *This was some kind of dream, a horrible nightmare*, I told myself, but no matter how hard I tried, I couldn't wake up.

Seconds later, I felt something tugging at the covers at the foot of my bed. I pulled the blankets and sheets over my head and held them tight. Then I remembered that I had stashed my pocketknife beneath my pillow. My hand was trembling as I slowly slid it between the sheet and pillowcase. As I took the knife in my hand, I felt tiny footfalls moving along the bed, ever so slowly, as if the doll were trying to creep up on me as I slept. And then I heard a sound that made my heart stand still—a slight jingling of bells.

I fumbled to open the pocketknife. The footsteps drew closer and closer, until I felt something tug at the blankets that surrounded my head. I tried to hold onto them but somehow the thing was stronger than I was and I could feel the covers slipping away. A deafening thunderstrike broke the silence, and with a scream, I threw back the covers and lashed out with my knife, flailing wildly in the darkness. I felt the blade tear through the thing's flesh and heard its body hit the floor.

When my parents returned home, they found me huddled in the corner of my room, curled in a fetal pose. On the floor next to the bed, my brother lay in a pool of his own blood. His throat had been slashed and his body lay lifeless and cold. The doll sat beside him, smiling his evil smile, laughing at me.

The patient finished his story, immobilized by thick leather restraints that shackled his wrists and ankles to the hospital bed. "That was twenty-two years ago, and I've been here ever since. The police said that my brother must have snuck into my room to scare me. I tried to tell them what had really happened—that the doll was alive, but no one would believe me. They said that I killed him, but it was the doll... *it was the doll,* and he's coming for me." The doctor stepped closer to examine a jagged series of scars lining the patient's arms and face, then jotted some notes on his chart. "They restrained me because they think I did this to myself, but it was the doll, and he's coming back tonight. You've got to believe me. You've got to get me out of here," his voice grew more excited. "They stabbed me with needles and drugged me and left me in this padded cell, alone in bleak darkness, with no way to defend myself." He struggled in vain against his bonds as the two doctors turned to leave. "Don't leave me here like this! Please," he begged, "don't leave me here *with him!*" But his cries fell upon unsympathetic ears as the heavy steel door slammed shut, leaving him alone in the solitude of his dark cell.

As the distant thunder erupted, lightning illuminated the dim corners of the room. Tears welled in his eyes as he heard the sound of jingling bells. The lightning flickered to reveal a small figure that had stepped forward from the shadows, then the room was engulfed in cruel darkness once more.

# THE LEGEND OF DARKLORE MANOR

*by Joseph Vargo*

*Along a dark, forsaken road,*
*There stands a stark and grim abode —*
*An old manor house looms black and tall,*
*To cast a grave and deathly pall—*
*Beyond the ancient wrought iron gate,*
*A thousand nightmares lie in wait —*
*For dark things dwell in this house of fear,*
*And none but the dead dare trespass here—*

Stories of haunted houses abound throughout America and Europe, but few can boast as many ghostly and unnatural occurrences as Darklore Manor, the abandoned Victorian mansion that once loomed over the town of Gloucester, Massachusetts, just up the coast from Salem. Strange and unbelievable tales have been passed down from the time of the earliest settlers to the region, spawning dark and ominous legends that have survived to this day. Native American tribes named the area "the place where shadows walk," and seldom ventured near the surrounding forests. It is also believed that the region was originally settled by citizens of Salem Village who fled the town during the infamous witch trials in 1692, and that the area became a haven for practitioners of black magic.

Whatever the true historical origins, it is a place where spirits of the dead do not rest easy, nor do they find release from their eternal sorrow. As for Darklore Manor, its history is a grim and tragic tale, steeped in darkness and blood.

The mansion was built by Edmund Darklore for his lovely young bride Delarosa during the end of the 19th century. Construction of the three-story, forty-room Victorian manor began in 1889 and was completed three years later. During the course of its construction, two stone masons were crushed to death beneath a wall of bricks when a hoist rigging mysteriously snapped in two.

Over the next forty years, a series of tragedies and deaths plagued those who would call Darklore Manor home. In 1941, the last of the Darklore bloodline, Damon Darklore, his wife Elizabeth and their daughter Belladonna vanished without a trace overnight, leaving the mansion deserted.

Abandoned and left to fall into disrepair, this once elegant manor began its decline into decay. Eventually, tales of ghostly sightings began to surface around the deserted mansion. Throughout the years there have been numerous reports of strange lights and sounds coming from inside the house. A dark form known as the "Shadow Man" has been sighted at the entrance gates. Another ghost, known as the "Lady in Black," is believed to be the spirit of Belladonna Darklore, and has been sighted wandering the manor grounds and halls. It is said that her dark form appears when the clock strikes the midnight hour.

So many rumors and tales have been told about the mansion and its ghosts over the years that it has become difficult to discern fact from fiction.

My name is Pamela Moore, and I am the last surviving person that knows the true legend of Darklore Manor.

My tale begins in 1967. I was twenty-four years old and had landed a job working as the personal assistant to a woman named

Sandra Faraday. Sandra was somewhat of a celebrity in certain circles. She had gained some notoriety as a psychic and spiritualist and was highly respected in the occult community. In addition to her paranormal research, she had written several articles on ghosts and the supernatural and she had hired me to help her assemble and edit a book of her collected essays. There was a strange contrast between my strict Catholic upbringing and Sandra's occult beliefs and skeptical views on religion. Although we didn't see eye to eye on certain spiritual matters, Sandra and I were as close as sisters. Many a night we sat up talking over a bottle of wine, discussing man's place in the cosmic design and debating concepts of the afterlife.

One Monday morning in late September I reported to Sandra's home bright and early for work. I had just returned to New York after visiting my parents in Pennsylvania. Sandra answered the door in her bathrobe and handed me a cup of coffee before I even stepped inside.

"You read my mind," I said, taking a sip of the freshly brewed java.

"That's what I do," she replied with a smile as she sauntered into the kitchen.

Despite what some people believed, Sandra couldn't actually read minds or foretell the future, but she definitely possessed an uncanny sense of intuition about people and places. She could tell things about a person simply by touching something that belonged to them and if she visited a place, she knew things about the people who lived there, even if they had died long ago.

I took a seat at the kitchen table as Sandra poured herself a cup of herbal tea. The latest issue of *Haunted Havens*, a pulp occult magazine, was sitting on the table. The magazine had run an interview with Sandra a few months earlier discussing several famous hauntings. In her typical straightforward style, Sandra didn't pull any punches. She bluntly voiced her opinion on the sites in question, stating which ones she thought were authentic and which ones were hoaxes, adding that she would have to visit the sites in person to get more accurate impressions from the spirits that dwelled there.

The article generated a lot of letters, mostly from people who applauded Sandra's honesty and professional scrutiny. In addition to a nominal payment, the publisher gave her a lifetime subscription to *Haunted Havens* as compensation for the interview.

"Take a look at this," she said, opening the magazine to an article titled "The Curse of Darklore Manor." A black and white photograph showed a decrepit Victorian mansion looming behind tall iron gates covered with withered vines. The stately manor looked imposing, to say the least.

"Darklore Manor? I've never heard of this place."

"It's in Massachusetts, near Salem—in a little seaport town named Gloucester." She pointed to a section of the article labeled Mysterious Deaths, and said "Here, read this part."

I picked up the magazine and began to read it aloud. "'On the night of November 27th, 1961, area businessman Theodore Thompson and his wife, Sharon, were killed in an automobile accident when their car crashed into a tree in front of the mansion. They were survived by their six-year-old son, Theo Jr., who told the police that his father swerved the car to avoid hitting a woman dressed in black who was standing in the middle of the road, directly in front of the gates leading to the house.

"'On March 13th, 1962, local councilman Richard Franklin was found hanged to death inside the manor. Although no note was found, the case was ruled a suicide. One curious footnote concerns the fact that Councilman Franklin was the last surviving member of the Brotherhood of Thule, a masonic order of town elders that was founded by Edmund Darklore.'" I looked at Sandra. "Is any of this stuff true?"

"Yes, and there's more," Sandra said, taking a sip of her tea. "The article claims that the mansion is the site of more than a dozen mysterious deaths. According to the story, these fatalities are believed to be connected to the occult rituals practiced by this mysterious Brotherhood of Thule."

"Sandra, you know how *Haunted Havens* likes to sensationalize their stories."

"I know. That was my first impression too, but I've been doing some research on this place and it all checks out. A letter written by Edmund Darklore's last surviving descendant, Damon Darklore, claims that his ancestors fell victim to a curse brought on by their own macabre delvings into the realm of black magic. According to popular accounts of the legend, the Darklores conducted arcane ceremonies involving ancient sacrificial rites within a secret chamber deep below the manor. Whether intentionally or by accident, they awakened an ancient evil which caused the plague of deaths surrounding the mansion throughout the years. The legend states that whatever was conjured forth not only claimed several human lives, but also stole the souls of those who died within the manor, leaving them cursed to haunt the mansion and grounds for eternity."

"Lovely."

"Yes, but that's not the best part. The story goes on to say that something unnatural still dwells there, lying in wait for unwary visitors, hungering for the blood of the living and the souls of the dead."

"Sounds a little melodramatic. You can't possibly be buying all of this."

"I know it all sounds pretty far-fetched, but I actually think this place is worth looking into. I've been having some strange dreams lately."

Among her many unexplainable abilities, Sandra's dreams were often prophetic. "Anything you'd care to share?" I asked.

"They're vague, but I'm in a very dark place, surrounded by shadowy figures. They're whispering to me, calling my name. They're trying to tell me something, but I can't understand what they're saying. I'm not sure if it's an invitation or some kind of a warning."

"How many times have you had the dream?"

"Twice in the past few nights. They began right after I got this." She withdrew a clear plastic sleeve from inside a large manila envelope. An old letter was sealed inside the protective cover. The aged parchment was yellowed and tattered at the fringes. The handwriting displayed an antiquated style that was elegant, yet masculine. A blood-red wax seal held an ornate letter D at the bottom.

"Is this what I think it is?"

Sandra nodded her head. "The genuine article. Go ahead and read it."

I carefully took the letter from her hand and began to read its grim contents.

*Woe befalls all who dwell within Darklore Manor, for those who have met their fate within this blighted place are cursed to forever wander its unhallowed halls. Within this sanctuary of shadows, the restless dead can find no surcease from their eternal suffering.*

*I have brought this curse upon myself, as did my ancestors before me. I hereby confess my guilt, for I have conspired in blasphemous acts and have committed grievous and ghastly deeds. And though I be the last of the Darklore bloodline, this curse shall not end with my death, for we have awakened a great darkness, and its unfathomable hungers cannot be quenched. May the Lord have mercy on my soul.*

*I implore you to heed my warning. Leave this place and never return, lest ye fall victim to the Darklore curse and are doomed to an eternity of suffering and sorrow.*

It was signed Damon Darklore.

"How did you get this?" I asked.

"Carl Weiss brought it over."

"The editor of *Haunted Havens*?"

"One and the same," she replied. "He wanted to see if I could

*Woe befalls all who dwell within Darklore Manor, for those who have met their fate within this blighted place are cursed to forever wander its unhallowed halls. within this sanctuary of shadows, the restless dead can find no surcease from their eternal suffering.*

*I have brought this curse upon myself, as did my ancestors before me. I hereby confess my guilt, for I have conspired in blasphemous acts and have committed grievous and ghastly deeds. And though I be the last of the Darklore bloodline, this curse shall not end with my death, for we have awakened a great darkness, and its unfathomable hungers cannot be quenched. May the Lord have mercy on my soul.*

*I implore you to heed my warning. Leave this place and never return, lest ye fall victim to the Darklore curse and are doomed to an eternity of suffering and sorrow.*

*—Damon Darklore*

get any impressions from the letter. He wouldn't tell me how he acquired it, but he said he had the writing checked against Damon Darklore's signature from an old land deed and he swears it's authentic."

"What did you tell him?"

"I got a very weird vibe from it. I've never felt anything quite like it before. I told him that I thought the legend was definitely something worth looking into, and he agreed. We started discussing the possibility of conducting a paranormal investigation of Darklore Manor."

"And?" I asked.

Sandra took a long sip of her tea, then smiled and asked, "How would you like to spend the night in a haunted house?"

I stared at her blankly, unable to respond. Sandra capitalized on my silence, using it as an opportunity to pitch her idea.

"Carl pulled some strings with the mayor of Gloucester. It's all set up. We'll have the run of the place for twenty-four hours. We'll document our findings and *Haunted Havens* will run it as a feature, promoting it as 'Sandra Faraday Spends the Night in a Haunted Mansion.' It'll be a great chapter for my book, not to mention all the publicity that something like this is bound to bring us."

"When is this all supposed to take place?" I asked.

"The day after tomorrow."

"What?"

"We've got to move quick on this thing. Carl wants it for his Halloween issue. It's only a four-hour drive from here. If we leave here early Wednesday morning, we can be there before noon.

"That won't give me much time to prepare."

"Here's my research notes," she said, sliding the manila envelope across the table. "I just need you to see what you can dig up on this Brotherhood of Thule."

"We'll need a cameraman to document everything."

"It's all been taken care of," Sandra replied with a reassuring grin, "I talked it over with Ronnie and he's in."

"You're really serious about this, aren't you?"

"No one's been inside the mansion for years. And no one's ever conducted an official paranormal investigation of the place. This could be really big. If there is something there, we'll be the first to document it. Worst case scenario, there's nothing there and we get to explore a cool old mansion and debunk a legend."

"Did you ever consider an even-worse case scenario?"

"Like what?"

"Like maybe this Darklore curse is real and we all die horrible deaths inside the house."

"That's the spirit," she said with a laugh, then asked "Are you in?"

Had I only told Sandra "no," I might have enjoyed a healthy and prosperous life, free from the horrors that now plague my nightmares. But even though I had some lingering reservations about joining her expedition into the domain of the supernatural, I was intrigued by the legend of Darklore Manor and I chose to satisfy my own morbid curiosity.

"I'm in," I said.

There are certain occasions when we find ourselves at a crossroad in our lives, presented with two choices, never knowing how one simple decision may drastically alter the course of our destiny. The wrong choice at such a juncture could be disastrous, setting into motion a series of events that inevitably lead to irreversible catastrophe. This was one such time.

Sandra had wasted no time in assembling her team to investigate the haunting. She had recruited her photographer friend Ron Cooke who, in turn, enlisted the services of a lighting and recording technician named Jake Martelli. The two of them had worked together on several professional ghost hunts in the past, exploring historical sites and graveyards in search of restless spirits.

Aside from being the star of the show, Sandra also acted as the producer and director, overseeing every minute detail of the investigation. My duties were perhaps the most mundane. After gathering the preliminary research, my job entailed penning an impromptu script for Sandra and taking shorthand notes to document everything we witnessed inside the manor. It was a compact but efficient squad with each member capable of juggling several duties.

The investigation was scheduled for September 27th. The plan was to spend the entire day and night inside the mansion then leave the next afternoon. Once the investigation was finished, Sandra and I had two days to write the article and get it to Carl Weiss just in time for his magazine's Halloween issue. It was a tight schedule, but we'd met tougher deadlines in the past.

Sandra and I planned to drive to Gloucester together, leaving early on the morning of the 27th. The guys would drive out in a separate car and meet us at the manor in the afternoon. The fact that it would be just the two of us girls making the trek together made it feel like a college road trip.

We hit the highway just before 7 a.m., avoiding the brunt of rush-hour traffic. As usual, Sandra insisted on driving, making me the designated navigator. As we drove along the east coast highway we shared some girl talk and laughs, then began to review the case.

"So what did you find out about the mysterious Brotherhood of Thule?" Sandra asked.

Consulting my notes, I began to read what I had discovered about the enigmatic sect. "The Thule Society was founded in Germany near the end of the Victorian era. According to legend, Thule was an island located somewhere in the far northern Atlantic Ocean. This mysterious and secluded isle was said to be the last outpost of an ancient advanced race of beings that inhabited the Earth long ago. These 'Ancients' or 'Masters,' as they were called, could be contacted through mystical rites and black magic and could enlighten and endow the initiated with supernatural abilities. Thule ceremonies involved ritual chants and sacrifices that would allow communication with the Ancients.

Membership into the inner circle of the Thule Society was closed to women, and for this reason certain sects were also known as the Brotherhood of Thule."

"Interesting."

"Do you believe any of it? I mean do you really think that this place is haunted, or that the Darklore curse is real?"

She stared out at the highway for a long moment, as if contemplating whether or not to reveal her true thoughts to me. Finally she confided, "I believe something's there. I'll admit that I have an uneasy feeling about going into that place."

"Why?"

"It's the dreams," she said quietly, "they've been getting stronger. I can see things clearer now. I'm inside an old house. It doesn't look or feel familiar, but I seem to know where every door and hallway leads. There's music playing—sort of a light childish melody—and I see a little girl in a scarlet dress. Her skin is white and smooth. She's all alone and I get this terrible feeling of sadness. There's a door that I can't open, and somehow I know that I should never open it, never step inside, but something is calling me from beyond the door. And then I see a man. He's tall and cloaked in shadows. I can never see his face, but he whispers to me, repeating the same name over and over again. He's calling to me, but it's not my name that echoes from his lips."

"What does he say?" I asked.

Sandra paused for a moment to compose her emotions, then whispered, "Belladonna."

We arrived in Gloucester just after 11 a.m. It was a quaint little town that reminded me of something out of a Norman Rockwell painting. The old-fashioned architecture of the buildings held a simple rustic charm. The town square was lined with curious little shops and red brick office buildings nestled together in a cozy setting. I couldn't imagine such a peaceful and inviting place harboring a mansion of horrors.

Sandra dropped me off at a local market store to grab some last-minute supplies then she headed to the police station to meet with the sheriff. Twenty minutes later she picked me up in front of the store.

"I spoke with the sheriff. He's meeting us here at 11:30 to drive out to the manor with us and let us in. He made us a copy of the mansion's floorplan. Ronnie and Jake got here about an hour ago and went on ahead to take some establishing shots of the mansion's exterior." As she spoke, Sandra used the car's rear-view mirror to fix her hair and apply a fresh coat of lipstick.

"So what's the sheriff like?"

"Tall, dark, handsome—not your type at all."

"I see."

"This is him now," Sandra said, nodding her head in the direction of an approaching police vehicle. "Just remember, Pammy, I saw him first."

The police car pulled alongside us and the sheriff got out and walked over to our vehicle. Sandra wasn't kidding. He was tall with dark hair and chiseled features. He looked to be somewhere in his mid-thirties, which would have made him right around Sandra's age.

"Sheriff Hill, allow me to introduce you to my trusted assistant, Pamela Moore."

"Nice to meet you, ma'am. Welcome to Gloucester." His husky voice matched his rugged good looks.

He quietly stared through the driver's side window, shifting his gaze between Sandra and I, as if sizing up our strength for what lay ahead. "Are you sure you know what you're getting yourselves into here?"

Sandra smiled and said, "We do this for a living. We have a very high threshold for fear."

There was a hint of skepticism in his eyes that felt vaguely insulting. After an uncomfortable moment of silence he returned Sandra's smile and gestured to the road behind him. "The mansion is about twelve miles from here, out along Old Salem Road. Just follow me."

The sheriff got back in his car and led us out of town. We trailed close behind him, heading south along a two-lane road that ran between a long stretch of dense woods and a rocky cliff overlooking the Atlantic shore. At times the narrow road veered dangerously close to the edge of the cliff and the tumultuous sea below. After several miles the road turned inland and the woods thinned to sparse patches of twisted trees and wild brush.

After another mile or so, the sheriff's car slowed to a crawl and turned down an old red brick drive. As we followed him along the overgrown trail, a distant shadow began to emerge from the surrounding cover of barren trees and tangled vines, and as we drew nearer my eyes beheld Darklore Manor for the first time.

A tall wrought iron fence surrounded the manor grounds and withered vines twisted in and out of the black gates, wrapping themselves around the rails and posts, blocking the view of the grim structure from the main road, completely isolating it from the world around it. The mansion loomed in the distance beyond the black gates, high on a hill overlooking a wide stretch of unkempt property overgrown with tall grass and thorny bramble.

The sheriff's car came to a halt alongside Ronnie's van, which was parked near the entrance gates. Sandra pulled in on the other side of the van and neither one of us moved or said a word as she threw the gearshift into park. We both sat speechless, staring at the nightmarish vision before us.

Standing three stories tall, the mansion was a magnificent and macabre relic from the past, ravished by time and tragedy. The stone and bricks that comprised the building's weathered facade had darkened nearly to black, casting a sinister taint over the ornate details of the elaborate masonry. Gothic columns framed the main entrance and supported a stone balcony surrounded by a parapet reminiscent of a medieval castle. Three pointed dormers crowned the mansion's heights and the peaks of each roof were topped with antique lightning rods that ended in tall iron spikes.

Narrow windows lined the edifice at sparse intervals, but the glass appeared solid black and seemed to absorb the light of the graying sky, rather than reflect it. The twisted trees and dead vines that clung to the mansion's perimeter gate added a final accent to the sense of menace and foreboding gloom that permeated the site.

We sat mesmerized by Darklore Manor's macabre hypnotic hold until a nearby clicking sound roused us from our trance. Ronnie had snuck up next to our car to snap a photo of us.

"Sorry," he laughed, "but I had to get a picture of your faces the first time you laid eyes on this place. Is this awesome, or what?"

Jake walked up alongside him and said, "We did the same thing when we first got here. We just sat there staring at it. This place is incredible."

Ronnie and Jake were an unlikely pair, but they had been friends for more than ten years and the two worked together like a well-oiled machine. They were both in their late twenties, but that's about where the physical similarity ended. Ronnie had a slender physique and thinning blonde hair. He never went anywhere without his camera, which he wore like a medal of honor on a strap around his neck. Over the years he had several showings of his photography in some fairly prestigious galleries. He was a true artist, and as such, he was somewhat eccentric.

Jake was an electrician by trade. He was the consummate professional and all-around workhorse. He was extremely resourceful and his powers of deductive reasoning allowed him to troubleshoot almost any problem. He had a stocky, muscular build that enabled him to haul hefty loads of equipment with ease. He was a good guy to have on your side if the going got tough.

As we got out of the car, the sky began to darken.

"Looks like rain," Jake said, nodding his head toward a patch of threatening clouds that loomed in the distance. "I think a storm's heading this way."

"Perfect." Sandra said with a laugh.

Ronnie reloaded his camera with a fresh roll of 35mm film,

then strapped on a large military backpack that he had filled with photographic equipment and various supplies. Jake hoisted two large satchels out of the van and slung one over each of his shoulders, then he pulled out a large cooler and set it on the ground. Sandra and I traveled light, bringing only our purses, a few blank notebooks and our case research files. As we gathered our luggage and prepared to embark on our excursion, the sheriff approached Sandra.

"So what do you think, Miss Faraday? It's not too late to turn back." The tone of his voice made it difficult to tell whether he was serious or kidding.

"Very impressive," Sandra replied. "The photos I saw don't do this place justice. It's a lot bigger than I thought it would be. I'm surprised that no one else is here. I expected the place to be swarming with curious locals. Something like this usually draws a pretty big crowd."

"We kept things kind of quiet. We didn't want to make a big fuss about it. I didn't think you'd want a major commotion out here."

"That was very thoughtful, Sheriff. Thank you." Her voice was sweet as sugar as she spoke to him. I turned my head and rolled my eyes behind her back and Jake chuckled.

The sheriff handed Sandra an old skeleton key and said, "This will get you inside the front door. After that, you're on your own."

"You're not going to chaperone us?"

"No," he replied with a nervous laugh, "I don't want to be in your way. I'll be right outside, making sure you're not disturbed. If you need me, just give me a holler. One of my deputies will take over for me tonight, but I'll be back here in the morning."

"You don't like this place much, do you, Sheriff?"

"I've only been inside the mansion once, five years ago, and that was enough for me. I'm not a superstitious person, at least I never used to be, but that was before I saw what this place could do to a man."

"You mean Richard Franklin, the councilman who hung

himself here?"

He looked at Sandra with a puzzled expression, as if he thought she were reading his mind.

"I saw the police report, Sheriff. It said you were the one who found his body."

"That's right. I was just a deputy at the time. I knew Richard. He was a good man—smart and stable. Something inside that place must've made him snap." The sheriff's stoic facial expression faded to a look of sorrow. "But that's in the past. Right now my main concern is you and your crew."

The sheriff checked his watch, then said, "You'll have daylight till about 8:30. After sundown, you'll need to use flashlights and lanterns. The electricity's been shut off for years, but the place still has candelabras in every room and hall. Just be careful not to set anything on fire. The old wood inside the manor is as dry as kindling. One careless match and the whole place will go up like a tinder box."

"You seem to know a lot about this place."

"Yeah. You can't grow up in Gloucester without knowing about Darklore Manor and the Darklore curse. Most people in town won't come anywhere near this place, except for a few curious kids."

"Why hasn't it been sold or demolished?"

"It's complicated. In the first place, nobody has ever made an offer to buy it—probably because of its history. Folks around here are kind of superstitious, and I can't say that I blame them. The city council doesn't want to spend the money to tear it down and nobody wants to build anything new on the land, so there it sits."

"One last question, Sheriff—does the house have a basement?"

"I take it you've heard the rumors about the secret chamber below the mansion."

"Does it exist?"

"Well," the sheriff began, then hesitated, "the manor doesn't have any cellar windows, and nobody's been able to find any doors leading to a lower level... but that doesn't mean there isn't one."

"What makes you say that?"

"The old blueprints of the mansion don't show anything beneath the main level, but Edmund Darklore was a mason and he made a lot of renovations to the mansion's interior in the 1920s. He allegedly constructed an ancestral crypt below the mansion where all their descendants are buried. According to the rumors, the Knights of Thule held their meetings down there." The sheriff shrugged his shoulders and added, "It might just be a rumor."

"Thanks. We'll see what we can find."

"I hope you know what you're getting yourself into here, Miss Faraday. Maybe you can do some good by finding the source of the problem. Maybe you and your team can set things right. Just be careful in there. The ghosts that haunt this place are real." His voice held a deadly serious tone.

"I appreciate the concern."

The sheriff walked up to the front gate and unlocked an old padlock that secured a heavy chain holding the gate shut.

Ronnie was taking a long drag off a cigarette as Sandra announced, "Smoke 'em if you got 'em, boys. Once we get inside, no more cigarettes."

"I know, boss," he replied, dropping the butt to the ground and twisting it into the dirt beneath his boot.

Jake approached Sandra, carrying a portable cassette recorder. "This is for you," he said, handing her the device. "You wear it like a purse and just turn it on and off with the microphone switch. The mike clips onto the strap, so it doesn't get in your way."

"Cool. Thanks, Jake." She slung the strap of the cassette recorder over her shoulder and checked the microphone for a good volume level. "Okay, people, let's get this show on the road."

Sandra stepped in front of the unlocked entrance gates and, as if on cue, a torrent of billowing thunderclouds rolled in to set an ominous backdrop behind the mansion's towering spires. The shutter of Ronnie's camera snapped away as Sandra turned on the hand-held microphone and began to recite her introduction.

"Welcome to Darklore Manor, where spirits of the dead do not rest easy, nor do they find release from their eternal sorrow. The history of this household is a grim and tragic tale, steeped in darkness and blood. My name is Sandra Faraday. Follow me as I explore the shadows of this forsaken dwelling in an attempt to uncover the macabre secrets buried long ago and confront the horrors that yet lurk within the confines of this haunted domain."

Sandra stepped toward the mansion's entrance gate and took hold of the latch, pulling one side of the gate open. "Beyond the rusted iron gates, overgrown with vines, a weathered cobblestone path leads up to the deserted manor house."

Twin gargoyles sculpted in the likeness of medieval griffons sat perched atop tall stone posts on either side of the gateway, guarding the manor house from unwanted guests. The grim statues glared down with lifeless eyes as we passed through the weathered gate. Sandra led the way and I was close behind her, followed by Ron and Jake, as we trod the timeworn cobblestones toward the looming manor house. With every step, the grim details of the mansion's exterior came into focus. The pitted surface of the dark bricks, the blistered paint, the cracked masonry and the black windows that watched our every move all echoed the neglect and pain that seemed to remain trapped within its walls.

Our solemn procession advanced slowly as we made our way along the path to a stone staircase that led up to the mansion's main entrance. As we ascended the steps, the wind began to pick up, forming a ghostly choir as it whistled through the forest of dead trees and tangled vines that surrounded the grounds.

When we reached the top of the staircase, the sound of distant thunder rumbled through the sky, sending a low, feral growl echoing across the heavens as we stood before the doors of the mansion. Ronnie snapped several close-ups as Sandra withdrew the ornate skeleton key from her pocket and slowly slid it into the tarnished keyhole. She turned the key in the lock and the heavy door squealed open. None of us spoke a word or moved an inch as we stared into the bleak shadows that permeated the manor's interior.

After a long moment of silence, Sandra resumed her ongoing monologue. "The entrance door creaks open wide, daring mortals to cross the threshold of the dead." Without further hesitation, she accepted the grim invitation, boldly stepping into the shadowy domain.

Ron and Jake were quick to follow, but I held back, contemplating my decision for a long moment. A voice deep inside me pleaded for me to turn around and retrace my steps to the safety of the world outside the mansion's gates, but another voice prodded me forward. I had come too far and there was no turning back now. With a lingering sense of trepidation, I entered Darklore Manor.

We stood in the entry foyer of the mansion, engulfed within an abyss of shadows and gloom. Hazy light filtered in through the narrow windows high above, providing dim illumination throughout the vast interior. Tarnished suits of medieval armor stood poised atop stone pedestals, flanking the sides of the foyer as it opened into the entrance hall. Their ancient helmets and breastplates were etched with intricate scrollwork and each dark knight held a large poleax clutched within its steel gauntlet. The silent sentinels cast an imposing presence as they kept their eternal vigil, standing watch over the entrance and acting as wards against all who would dare to intrude upon their forlorn domain.

"First things first," Sandra said, stepping back toward the open entryway. She took hold of the heavy door and slammed it closed behind us then locked it with the key, sealing us inside the manor.

"Is that really necessary?" I asked.

"We need to secure the perimeter. We can't have any distractions and I don't want any uninvited guests sneaking in here during our investigation." Sandra slipped the key into her jacket pocket. "If anybody wants to leave, just say so, but we're all professionals and we only have access to this place for 24 hours, so unless we have some kind of emergency, that door stays locked until noon tomorrow." She walked back past us and headed into the main entrance hall, passing between the black suits of armor that towered high above her.

"Don't worry," Jake whispered, flashing me a consoling smile, "if we really need to get out of here fast, we can just borrow one of those battle axes and make our own door." He nodded his head toward one of the knights and my eyes focused on the massive double-headed blade clutched in its grasp.

As Ron took some establishing shots of the foyer, Jake escorted me past the grim guardians. The sounds of the approaching storm grew louder and sporadic lightning flashes were followed by violent thunderstrikes that sent reverberations throughout the manor. Sandra walked to the middle of the entrance hall and slowly turned in a circle, surveying the immense room that surrounded her. Dust covered the floor and cobwebs hung from the ceiling, draping the gloomy interior beneath decades of neglect.

Sandra continued her audio documentary. "A veil of darkness shrouds the vast interior of the once elegant manor. For years no living soul had desecrated this sanctuary of shadows." Her voice echoed throughout the chamber as she spoke.

The interior of the house was a remarkable example of Victorian Gothic architecture. It had withstood the cruel years to survive as a grim monument to fallen memories. Gothic columns supported stone archways that led to wings on either side of the entrance hall. At the far end of the room, a grand staircase swept upward to a landing then split-off to the left and right. Twin griffons, matching the ones that guarded the entrance gates, sat perched upon the banisters on either side of the main staircase. The stone beasts gazed across the hall, their glaring eyes locked upon the armored sentinels that stood opposite them.

"It's magnificent," Ronnie said, snapping a series of shots of the room. "What I wouldn't do to own a place like this."

"It would probably cost a small fortune just to renovate it," I joked.

"I wouldn't touch a thing," Ronnie replied, "I'd leave it just the way it is."

Jake stared up into the canopy of cobwebs that hung over our heads, saying, "Yeah, well, you might want to dust once in a while."

Sandra began walking toward the archway that led to the south wing. "The dining room should be this way. We can set up our base of operations there."

We followed her through the arch and down a paneled corridor lined with oil paintings. Grim faces stared out from shadowy portraits. Their eyes seemed to follow us along the hallway as Sandra led us into the dining room.

A large banquet table filled the center of the room and ten high-backed chairs lined the sides of the table. Two tall candelabras, covered in cobwebs, rested on the table amidst a bouquet of long-dead flowers. A fireplace adorned the center of one wall and a large oil painting above the mantel depicted Darklore Manor as it looked when it was first built. A sad testament to lost dreams of the past, the painting was a bitter reminder of the lives that once flourished within the mansion's walls before tragedy took hold.

Jake set his cooler down on a worn Persian rug, saying, "There's water, soda and sandwiches, in case anyone gets hungry or thirsty." Then he proceeded to remove the satchels that hung over his shoulders and began meticulously emptying their contents onto the dining room table. He had brought an impressive selection of hand-held electronic devices, including thermometers, magnetometers, electrostatic detectors, and a few other gadgets he had designed himself.

Outside, the storm was now fully overhead. Rain pelted the leaded glass windows and the sound of crashing thunder split the calm at irregular intervals. Sandra stared out through a tall bay window as lightning ripped across the sky. "The storm put a serious damper on our daylight. We'll need to use the lanterns and flashlights."

“No problem, boss,” Ronnie said, “we came prepared for anything this house can throw at us.” He unstrapped his backpack and opened it to retrieve several flashlights and votive candles from amidst his stockpile of film and batteries. “Jake’s got all the heavy-duty stuff, but we probably won’t need to break out the lanterns and emergency lights till nightfall.” Ronnie handed me a flashlight, then lit one of the candles and set it on the table.

While the boys began gearing up, Sandra pulled out half a dozen pages of floorplans and spread them out over the dining room table, studying them intently like a general forming a plan of attack.

Ronnie reloaded his camera with a fresh roll of film and removed a second camera from a leather case.

“Two cameras?” I asked.

“Yes, ma’am,” he said, holding up the camera he had been using, “this one’s loaded with low-speed film to capture things in their natural gloomy setting.” He picked up the second camera and strapped it around his neck over the first one. “And this baby’s got a 300-watt flashbulb attachment to catch anything that’s hiding in the dark.”

“You’re dealing with professionals here, ma’am,” Jake said as he donned a hard hat with a built in headlamp. He gave me a wink and strapped on a utility belt that carried his array of gadgets and tools.

“Very impressive,” I said, “but the next one who calls me ma’am gets their name misspelled in the *Haunted Havens* article.”

Sandra stood at the head of the table and addressed the group. “Is everybody ready?”

“All set, boss,” Ronnie replied. Jake and I nodded our heads to agree.

“All right. You know the rules, people—stick together, stay in pairs, and don’t go wandering off alone. We’ll investigate each floor one at a time, starting with the ground floor and working our way up. The grande hall should be right through those doors across the entryway.” She placed her finger on a large room on the floorplan. "Let's start there, then work our way through the rest of the north wing."

Sandra slung the strap of the tape recorder over her shoulder then led us out of the dining room. As we made our way along the corridor, our flashlights and footsteps seemed to create sights and sounds that played tricks on our imaginations. Eerie chattering noises echoed around us and dark shapes appeared to stir and move in the distance.

Sandra resumed her audio documentary. "Within the confines of Darklore Manor, strange sounds echo like whispers from the corner of every room and shadows seem to shift with every step."

We made our way beneath the arch that led to the north wing and stood before the entrance to the grande hall. Twin doors made of dark wood were carved with intricate filigree that twisted around the framework in a serpentine design. Jake took hold of the brass doorknobs and looked at Sandra. She gave him a nod and he pulled the doors open.

The immense chamber was a lavish testament to Darklore Manor's decadent past and former grandeur. Cobwebs draped across the ceiling, covering several crystal chandeliers and cascading low into the hall. A magnificent fireplace hearth was set into the far wall between two tall windows. The mantel was supported by twin caryatids sculpted in the form of devilish satyrs. Their leering faces seemed to laugh with glee as their clawed fingers clutched the heavy stone mantel above their heads. The floor was made of black marble, and although it was difficult to discern beneath the thick coat of dust, an inlaid pattern of golden tiles formed a central design in the polished stone.

A balcony framed by an ornate marble railing circumvented the upper area of the room. Ronnie sprinted up the staircase that led to the surrounding loft and began to take some shots from the elevated vantage point. After snapping a few photos, he called down to us. "You guys really need to come up here and see things from this perspective."

We ascended the curving staircase and stood atop the balcony, gazing out over the ballroom floor. The design that adorned the marble floor was plain to see from the heights of the balcony. It formed a pattern of a seven-pointed star inside a surrounding circle of arcane symbols.

"What do you make of that?" Ron asked.

"It's a talisman design," Sandra replied, "most likely a symbol of power. I've seen similar mystical designs in occult books from the Middle Ages, but I don't recognize the outer symbols."

I made a crude sketch of the design as Ronnie snapped several photos of the floor.

Sandra voiced her thoughts as she looked out over the opulent room. "Edmund Darklore was obviously a very wealthy and successful man. I'd be curious to see the list of famous people that he entertained in this room."

"Shhh, listen," Ron interrupted. "Do you hear that?"

As we looked down from the balcony into the grande hall, the faint sound of music seemed to emanate from the chamber below. It lasted for a few seconds then faded away beneath the sounds of the ongoing storm.

"I could swear that I heard music," Ronnie whispered. "It sounded like..."

"A waltz," Sandra finished his sentence. "I heard it, too." She waved her hand through the air to the rhythm of the ghostly melody, then turned her cassette recorder on to chronicle her observation. "Eerie melodies still linger and echo throughout the grande hall. Decayed remnants of the forgotten past weave a haunting tapestry of a former splendor lost to the ravages of time."

Jake checked his instruments for fluctuations in the temperature and electromagnetic field in the room, then said, "I'm getting something." He turned and leaned out over the railing. "Look," he whispered, directing his flashlight beam toward the center of the floor.

A misty vapor had begun to materialize in the middle of the

room. At first it appeared to be little more than a wisp of dark smoke, but it quickly increased in size and density. We all stood in silence, watching the shapeless mass as it floated in the air a few feet above the ground.

"This is incredible," Jake whispered. "It's an actual manifestation. I can't believe we're seeing this."

Ronnie's camera clicked away as he captured several shots of the ghostly vapor hovering over the ballroom floor. The mist slowly began to rise and as it did, it drifted toward us, moving closer and closer until it hung suspended in the air between the four of us. It looked like a writhing cloud of smoke, nearly two feet in diameter with tendrils of dark mist slowly swirling throughout its shifting form. As I gazed upon the eerie sight before me, a strange feeling of sadness swept over me.

Sandra reached toward the ghostly vapor, but before she could touch it, the mist drifted off toward the outer wall. It stopped before a set of double doors at the rear of the balcony then faded from sight.

"Follow it," Sandra said.

Jake opened the balcony doors, and as he did, we caught sight of the ghostly mist once more, slowly floating along down the second floor hallway.

Sandra started after it, whispering into her microphone. "A spectral mist seems to dance through the cobweb-strewn corridors."

We trailed a few steps behind the eerie vapor as it slowly led us down a long hallway lined with portraits. When it neared the end of the hall, it dissolved into the surrounding shadows.

"That was... amazing," Jake exclaimed. "What do you think it was? An apparition—or possibly ectoplasmic residue?"

"It doesn't matter," Ronnie replied. "I got some great shots of it, whatever it was. Once these pictures are developed, we'll have genuine photographic proof of a paranormal entity. Do you know what that means? This will be groundbreaking."

"You still won't convince the die-hard skeptics," Sandra added, looking around curiously. "Does anyone else smell that? It's kind of sweet, like flowers or perfume."

Although its source was a mystery, the aroma was undeniable. The four of us turned our heads to face various directions, inhaling deeply as we tried to identify the unknown fragrance that lingered in the air.

"It's lavender," I said at last, recognizing the scent from my youth.

"Interesting," Sandra uttered beneath her breath.

"What do you think it means?" I asked.

She glanced around the corridor, scanning the paintings that surrounded us. "I think something in this house is trying to communicate with us. I think it led us here for a reason."

As we stood amidst the portraits that lined the hall, the somber faces of elderly men scowled from the shadows of pitch black canvases, and beautiful women, each with a similar melancholy expression, gazed out from beneath veils of cobwebs and dust. Sandra stopped before the painting of a middle-aged man with a stern cast to his dark eyes. A bronze plaque set into the bottom of the frame was inscribed with the name "Damon Darklore." She stood for a long while, intently staring at the portrait as if she were searching his rigid face for a clue to resolving the dark mysteries of the mansion.

Ronnie came up beside her and squinted at the name plaque below the painting. "So, this was the last owner of Darklore Manor, eh? He doesn't look too friendly."

Without taking her eyes off the painting, Sandra replied, "According to the legend, he and his wife and daughter just disappeared one night twenty-six years ago and the mansion has stood abandoned ever since."

Ronnie lowered his voice. "I gotta tell you, Sandy, I get a bad vibe from this place. There's something very wrong here. If I can sense it, I know you can, too."

"I know. I felt it as soon as I stepped through the entrance gates.

The energy is even stronger inside the house. It's heavy, and oppressive. I can feel its weight bearing down on me. There's definitely a presence here, and it's not just ghosts—there's something else, something ancient and malevolent."

As Sandra and Ron continued their discussion, my attention was suddenly drawn to a door at the end of the hall and I felt strangely compelled to investigate the chamber. I cautiously made my way to the doorway and peeked inside to discover what seemed to be a child's room. A plush single bed was framed by an exquisite hand-carved headboard adorned with Celtic knotwork. Dark velvet curtains were drawn closed over the windows, effectively blocking any shred of sunlight from entering the room. Paintings of ravens hung on either side of an ornate mirror attached to a mahogany vanity table.

I stepped inside the room to examine things more closely. A small perfume bottle rested on the vanity, covered in dust. I lifted the crystal stopper and raised the bottle to my nose but could barely detect a trace of the original scent in the decades-old mixture. I wiped the dust off the label to reveal that the fragrance it held was lavender. As I replaced the bottle on the vanity, I noticed an odd bare spot in the dust beside it. An oval shape on the counter top, roughly six inches wide, seemed to betray the fact that something had recently been removed from the spot.

As I stood contemplating the odd impression, a chill swept down my spine, and I felt the eerie sensation that I wasn't alone in the room. I glanced around the dim chamber, but there was no one there. Suddenly, I caught a glimpse of two small eyes staring at me from beneath a thick layer of cobwebs across the room. At first I was somewhat startled by the sight of the small figure that sat on the dresser, silently watching me, but as I slowly crept toward it, I could see that it was merely a child's doll, fashioned in the likeness of a little girl. Its face held an expression of sorrow and its unblinking eyes glistened with an eerie red glow as they reflected the light of my flashlight. Brushing aside the cobwebs, I examined it closer. It was draped in a red velvet dress and its porcelain face and hands were covered with a network of fine cracks. The doll's black hair was twisted into braids that were tied off with scarlet ribbons to match her dress.

"Sandra," I called out, "come in here."

Within seconds she was at the door. "What did you find?"

"Take a look at this," I said, holding my flashlight over the forsaken toy.

She stepped closer to get a better look at it. The doll's red eyes seemed to glare at us, as if there were some measure of consciousness lurking behind them. Neither one of us touched it as we examined it.

"Didn't you tell me you had a dream about a little girl with white skin who was wearing a red dress?" I asked.

"That's right," she said, "but in the dream, she was alive."

Sandra scanned the dresser with her flashlight beam. A book of nursery rhymes rested on the dresser beside the doll. She picked it up and flipped though its dusty pages to where a scarlet bookmark held a page with a handwritten poem.

Sandra studied the short verse intently then switched her microphone on to record her findings. "A child's poem written in a book of nursery rhymes harbors a sinister invocation." She paused for a moment, then began to read the verse aloud.

*Sandman, come to me tonight,*
*Comfort me till morning light—*
*As darkness falls and shadows loom,*
*I bid you welcome to my room—*
*Rest your bones beside my bed,*
*Lay your hands upon my head—*
*Cast your spell of slumber deep,*
*And stay beside me as I sleep—*
*If I should die before I wake,*
*I grant to you my soul to take—*

As she recited the final words of the macabre poem, an eerie melody broke the deathly silence. The faint chimes of a music box echoed from some distant part of the house. The ghostly refrain drew us out into the hallway where Ronnie and Jake were standing. Ronnie pointed down the main stairway, letting us know that the music was coming from somewhere on the first floor.

Sandra had left her microphone on to record what we were hearing and as she stood at the top of the staircase she added a bit of commentary. "From somewhere in the distance, a music box plays a haunting refrain."

We quietly made our way down the stairs and followed the hypnotic melody as it drew us toward the south corridor. The ghostly music led us through the tall archway and past the dining room. With each step we took, the chimes seemed to be slowing, as if the music box were winding down. As silently as possible, we approached a door near the far end of the hall. The eerie melody, which had slowed to a crawl, seemed to be emanating from inside the room. Sandra took hold of the handle and threw open the door, and as she did, the music stopped.

We stood in the doorway of a magnificent private library, awestruck and spellbound within the deathly hush. Tall bookcases were built into the oak-paneled walls and lavish works of art were displayed prominently throughout the chamber.

Sandra stepped inside the room, and as she did, she resumed her audio narrative. "The ghostly melody has led us to a library where the walls are lined with arcane relics and shelves of dusty books."

Heavy drapes covered the windows, muffling the sounds of the ongoing downpour and filtering the violent lightning flashes to a subdued flicker. A life-size statue of the goddess Athena stood on a marble pedestal just inside the chamber door. Her face was masked beneath an ancient helmet and her bronze shield bore the loathsome head of the gorgon, Medusa.

Ronnie snapped a quick photo of the imposing chamber before

setting foot across the threshold. After a moment of hesitation, he followed Sandra into the shadowy domain with Jake and myself trailing a few steps behind. The library seemed more like the grand showroom of a museum than a simple repository for books. Winged gargoyles leered down from gothic sconces set into the four corners of the room. Their monstrous faces were twisted into ferocious snarls, creating a sense of foreboding menace as they silently watched over the chamber. A majestic grandfather clock stood behind a veil of cobwebs in an arched alcove to our left. Its golden pendulum hung deathly still and its hands stood frozen in time at precisely one minute before twelve. A large globe of the world was supported on a pedestal beside an antique desk, piled high with books. Medieval broadswords and battle axes hung prominently displayed on the dark paneled wall behind the desk, forming an intimidating backdrop.

Near the center of the room, a leather sofa and matching chairs were arranged around a table in front of an ornate stone fireplace. A tall portrait depicting an elderly man wearing full Masonic regalia hung above the mantel. He stared down over the room like a ruthless monarch coldly surveying his conquered empire. There was little room for doubt that the painting portrayed the grand architect of Darklore Manor and all that had transpired within—the enigmatic Edmund Darklore.

Other paintings depicted classic scenes from ancient mythology. Beautiful Valkyries rode horses through the sky, transporting fallen warriors to the halls of Valhalla, and voluptuous sirens beckoned seductively to ancient mariners on a turbulent sea. A large framed canvas chronicled Lucifer's fall from Heaven, depicting a battle between angels and demons in lavish detail.

The shelves were filled with a treasury of rare books and strange artifacts from various cultures throughout history. A Mayan sundial rested on a stand surrounded by Native American totems, and jade dragons from the Orient shared a shelf with arcane relics from Tibet and India. A human skull covered with scrimshaw designs sat beside the sculpted effigy of the dark goddess Kali, and other pagan idols stared out from shadowy alcoves that lined the surrounding walls.

At the far end of the room, a pair of obsidian statues depicting Egyptian gods stood on the central shelf of a tall bookcase.

Sandra approached the sculptures, quietly studying them beneath her flashlight's glow. "Anubis and Osiris," she whispered, "the lords of the dead." A golden jewelry box, untouched by cobwebs, rested between the statues.

Sandra pondered the curious scene. "This seems a little out of place, doesn't it?" She rested her fingertips on box's oval lid and closed her eyes, as if she were meditating upon it. After a few seconds, she opened her eyes and gently lifted the jewelry box from its resting place. Examining it closely, she discovered a small key protruding from the base. She turned the key, twisting it round several times, then set the golden coffer back on the shelf and lifted the lid. The silence was broken once more as the eerie melody that had drawn us to the library began again.

As the hypnotic chimes of the music box rang out, I noticed that the oval shape of the coffer matched the bare spot in the dust that I had seen in the bedroom upstairs.

Sandra squinted at the bookcase in front of her. "So why did you bring us here?" she quietly mused, as if she were thinking out loud.

She ran her fingers along the edge of the bookcase, where the tall shelf protruded slightly. Grabbing hold of the frame, she pulled it toward her and the entire bookcase creaked away from the wall, revealing a secret doorway hidden behind it.

The concealed door was made entirely of bronze and a strange insignia adorned its tarnished center. The emblem showed a shield with crossed swords surrounded by an inscription that seemed to be written in Nordic runes. Sandra scanned the door with her flashlight, studying the engraved crest and as she did, I jotted the runic letters down in my notebook. Ronnie leaned in to photograph Sandra, capturing the moment as she stood before the mysterious barrier. She brushed her fingers over the tarnished surface until they came to rest upon a narrow slit cut into the center of the design.

"It's a keyhole," she said.

She quickly withdrew the front door key from her jacket pocket and tried it in the lock. She struggled as she attempted to twist it back and forth, but she couldn't turn it in either direction. Satisfied that the key didn't fit the lock, she slipped it back into her pocket and turned to Jake. "Do you think you can find a way to open this?"

Jake examined the surrounding crevices, pushing on the door and knocking on various parts of the frame. After a few futile minutes he conceded. "There's no hinges on this side and the damn thing's solid as a rock. Unless we find the key that fits this lock, we're gonna need a bulldozer to get it open."

"Where do you think it might lead?" I asked. "Maybe to a private study or den?"

Sandra returned her gaze to the crossed swords and shield on the insignia. "When the sheriff mentioned the Thule Society, he referred to them as the 'Knights of Thule.' I think this might be the entrance to their meeting room."

"Wasn't that supposed to be underground, in some sort of family burial crypt?" Ronnie asked.

"Exactly," Sandra replied. "There must be a key to this door somewhere in this house. Let's see if we can find it."

We turned our attention to investigating the library and over the course of the next hour we searched the numerous shelves and drawers looking for the elusive key, or any clue to its whereabouts. More than once Sandra seemed lost in a distant reverie as she examined several of the books and various other strange and dark wonders the room held.

The guys had retrieved some supplies from the dining room and sat at the central table gearing up for round two. Jake was systematically replacing the batteries in all the flashlights, ensuring that each one achieved maximum brightness. Ronnie sat opposite him, changing the film in his cameras with the deadly earnestness of a gunfighter loading his six-shooters before a showdown. Their dedication to their work was matched only by their skill and efficiency.

I decided that they had earned a mild compliment. "You guys make a great team."

"Yeah," Ron laughed. "He blazes a trail into the Stygian depths and I chronicle everything for posterity. Unfortunately, more often than not, he gets us lost and it's up to me to try to find our way back, usually in the dark."

"I beg your pardon." Jake feigned indignation. "Who led us out of that maze of catacombs beneath that sanitarium in Providence?"

"Who led us down there and got us lost in the first place?"

"Again, I ask—who got us out?"

"That was one time, and you got lucky."

"Maybe," he said, "but if I had my choice between being good, or being lucky, I'd rather be lucky." Jake flashed a devilish smile and gave me a wink.

Their humorous bickering lightened the mood in the dreary chamber. I walked over to Sandra who stood in a distant corner leafing through an old book of Norse mythology. Scanning the titles on the nearby shelf, I noticed that the entire bookcase was lined with aged tomes dedicated to a variety of esoteric topics. Secret societies, alchemy, black magic, witchcraft, talismans, necromancy, voodoo, thaumaturgy and mystical relics were but a few of the titles among the hundreds of arcane books that filled the tall shelf.

"This Edmund Darklore seems to have had more than just a passing interest in the occult," I said. My eyes came to rest on a large black book in the midst of the case. It was inscribed with faded gold letters that read Holy Bible. "That's odd," I said, brushing my fingers over the dusty spine. "He doesn't strike me as a religious man." I removed the heavy book from its resting place. "This doesn't seem to fit in with the other books on this shelf. It doesn't make sense."

"That's what I thought, at first," Sandra said, taking the Bible from my hands. "I was certain that it would be hollow and I'd find an old skeleton key hidden inside it, but it's just a regular book." She flipped through the pages to demonstrate that there was nothing concealed within it, then set it back on the shelf between the other books. "But now I think I understand why it's on this shelf. Look at the paintings and artifacts in this room. I don't think he was viewing the Bible as a religious tome, I think he was studying it as a collection of myths. All great mythologies of the world have some basis in truth. I think he was investigating the legends of various cultures throughout history, maybe looking for similarities, or myths that overlap. It's actually quite fascinating."

"And yet, after all his research, he put his faith in this Brotherhood of Thule?" I asked.

"Kind of makes you wonder why, doesn't it?"

"I'm sure he had some mad rationale for it," I said smugly.

"I don't think he was crazy. There's an old proverb that says we worship the gods that answer our prayers."

I glanced around at the extravagant works of art that filled the opulent chamber. "Well, from the look of things, I'd say that his gods were very good to him."

Sandra grinned. "He was obviously very passionate about the arts." She walked along the wall of books and gestured to the next set of shelves. "This entire bookcase is devoted to sculpture, painting, music and architecture." She proceeded to the neighboring bookcase and said, "This one's filled with classics of literature."

I perused the titles. The impressive collection contained several extremely rare books including leather bound works of Dante and Shakespeare and first editions of Byron and Poe. "This collection is amazing," I uttered. "The books on this one shelf alone must be worth a small fortune."

Sandra stepped over to the desk and began to examine the piles of dusty tomes that covered its surface. She lit a tall candelabra that resided amidst the crooked stacks, then took a seat behind the desk.

I pulled up a chair in front of her and sat down. "I wanted to ask you something—it's been on my mind for the past few hours."

"All right," she said, giving me her full attention.

"When we first got here, inside the manor, you led us straight to the dining room. You didn't look around or check the floorplan, or even hesitate for one second. How did you know where to go? And how did you know where that secret door was hidden?"

Sandra offered a slight smile then lowered her voice to reply. "Remember me telling you about my dreams—the ones where I'm inside an old house and everything seems familiar, like I've been there before?"

"Are you telling me that this is the house you've been dreaming about?"

"Yes. This is the house... and that's the door," she said, nodding her head toward the bronze barrier, "the one that should never be opened."

I stared at the foreboding doorway, and as I did I imagined a legion of hellish demons lying in wait just beyond its sealed threshold, biding their time till the infernal gateway was opened once again. As my mind drifted, I was startled out of my daydream by a disturbing sound—an innocent, childlike melody that gave me cause to shudder each time I heard it. The music box had suddenly begun to play once more.

Ronnie and Jake sprang to their feet and crept toward the source of the sound. Jake took hold of the bookshelf that had concealed the secret door and swung it shut, allowing us to see the front of the case. The music box still rested upon the central shelf, but the lid which had been left closed now stood open.

The eerie chimes rang out their haunting refrain, but this time when the music reached the chorus, a child's voice lightly joined in the melody. Sandra stepped forward and gently closed the lid and the music and singing stopped.

Sandra scoured the room with her gaze. "You needn't fear us," she said. "We're here to help you... we're listening... tell us your story... make us understand." She began to slowly walk around the library. "I know this was your home, but you're not alive anymore... you have to leave this place."

Suddenly, an icy chill swept through the room. Sandra winced, closing her eyes and recoiling, as if she had been struck by some unseen force. She began breathing heavily then started speaking in a quivering whisper. "Darkness," she said, "terrible darkness and sorrow." Tears welled in her eyes. "Eternal blackness... the sinners must be punished. He answered my prayers and told me what had to be done. Forgive me... forgive me."

Sandra opened her eyes and tears streaked down her cheeks.

"Are you all right?" I asked. "What happened?"

Sandra shook her head from side to side. "It was horrible. I've never felt anything like that."

"What did you feel?"

"Death... sorrow and death. It's all around us here." She slowly stepped to the library door, saying, "Follow me."

Walking as if in a trance, Sandra led us out of the room and around the corner to a narrow corridor adorned with the pictures of children. She stopped before an ornate oval frame and brushed the cobwebs aside to reveal the portrait of a beautiful young girl cast in shades of sepia. The girl was dressed entirely in black, as if she were attending a funeral when the photograph had been taken. Her dark eyes conveyed a sad expression as she gazed longingly outward from the faded picture. An inscribed plaque below the portrait read "Belladonna."

"It was her," Sandra whispered, "Belladonna Darklore—but there were other voices as well. Her family is dead, but their restless spirits are trapped within these walls. They're all here, inside this house."

Belladonna

As I stared at the solemn portrait of Belladonna, I felt a deep sympathy for her poor lost soul.

Sandra continued her account. "She said that the sinners had to be punished, and that someone answered her prayers."

"Who?" I asked.

"The Sandman," she whispered.

"Who or *what* is the Sandman?" Jake asked.

"It was in the poem," I replied, "in the book upstairs."

Sandra turned to Ronnie and said, "There's a book of nursery rhymes in the upstairs bedroom that Pam and I were in. Bring it to me. There's an old doll in that room, too. I need you to get some good photos of it." She glanced at Jake and said, "Go with him."

As the guys hustled off on their mission, Sandra and I walked back to the library. The storm had subsided somewhat, but occasional bursts of lightning flickered across the dark velvet drapes. The menagerie of statues that stood in various poses throughout the dim chamber cast eerie shadows in the light of the candelabra. Returning to the desk, we resumed our seats. Sandra removed her cassette recorder and set it down between two stacks of books, then leaned back in her chair.

I began the conversation, curious as to her thoughts on all that had transpired in the mansion. "So I take it you're convinced that this place is really haunted."

"Definitely, but this isn't a simple haunting. There's something more going on here."

"Like what?" I asked.

"I think we're being manipulated. Ever since we got here, we've been led around like sheep."

"By whom? Or should I ask by *what*?"

"I get a strong feeling that there's more than one force at work here. Something terrible happened in this house. The last of the Darklores didn't just abandon their home. They were murdered. Their spirits are trapped here, which makes me suspect that their bodies are somewhere within these walls as well." She stared past me, fixing her gaze upon the bookcase that concealed the secret passage. "I think a lot of answers lie on the other side of that door."

"Is that what your intuition tells you?" I asked.

"It's more than just simple intuition, Pam." Sandra leaned forward so she was close enough to reach the candelabra, then said, "Watch." She extended her right hand over the tall candles, holding her fingertips a few inches above the flame. "I can't see anything touching my fingers, but I can feel the heat of the fire. The closer I get to the source, the stronger the sensation." She waved her fingers through the flame and smiled as I flinched. "It's the same with our other senses, even the ones that we don't fully understand. Some of us are just more sensitive to the unseen world that surrounds us. Our perceptions are different, that's all. It doesn't mean that things you can't see aren't real. The realm of the paranormal really does exist."

"I get the feeling that you only brought me along on this excursion to try to convert me to your way of thinking."

"I'm just trying to expose you to some experiences that will open your mind to other possibilities. Why do you have such a hard time accepting all of this?"

"It's just difficult," I said. "I've lived my entire life with certain beliefs and I guess that until I see undeniable proof to the contrary, I'll always be a little skeptical."

"How can you still be skeptical after all you've experienced in this house? What about the apparition in the ballroom? We all witnessed it. How can you deny the existence of something you've seen with your own eyes?"

"I don't deny that I saw something... I'm just not sure what it was."

"You heard the music." Sandra gestured her hand toward the music box on the bookshelf.

"There could be a logical explanation for it."

Sandra shook her head in disgust. "Now you're making excuses."

"Maybe I am," I said solemnly. "I guess it's only natural to want to cling to what feels safe."

Before Sandra could respond, our conversation was interrupted by yelling in the distance. It was Jake, shouting Sandra's name. His voice sounded muffled, but it carried a sense of urgency. We bolted out of the library and hurried toward the sound of his voice. His yells led us into the entrance hall.

Jake was standing at the top of the main staircase. "Up here, quick," he said.

We sprinted up the stairs to the second floor hallway.

"Where's Ronnie?" Sandra asked.

"This way," he said, then turned and led us down the dim corridor to the far end of the hall. Ronnie was sitting on the floor with his back against the wall, just outside the bedroom door. He seemed dazed and shaken, as if he had witnessed something that made him question his own sanity.

"What's wrong?" Sandra asked.

"This whole place is wrong." Ronnie's voice trembled. "Like I told you before, there's something seriously, *seriously* wrong here."

"Settle down, Ronnie. Just tell me what happened."

He took a deep breath to regain a portion of his composure, then began to tell his tale. "I was in the bedroom. I found the book of nursery rhymes right where you said it would be, but I didn't see any doll. I looked all over the room, but I couldn't find any trace of it.

"I grabbed the book and started heading back when I saw a small figure in the hall outside the door. It was the doll—standing there in her little red dress, her white face covered with tiny cracks, her soulless eyes staring right through me.

"I thought you were screwing with me—like you had put it there as a joke. I took a step toward it…" He paused. "And, I swear... the thing took a step toward me."

As incredible as his words sounded, Sandra gave no reaction to his bizarre claim. "Go on," she said.

"I slammed the door shut and held it closed. I actually said a prayer to try to make the thing go away. After a few minutes, Jake knocked on the door and I opened it to let him in. I checked the hallway, but it was empty. The doll was nowhere to be found." When he finished telling his story, he looked Sandra directly in the eye and said, "I didn't imagine it. I know what I saw."

Sandra shot Jake a scolding look and said, "Where were you while all this was happening? You guys were supposed to stick together."

"I know... I'm sorry. I was taking some thermal readings in the hall just outside the room and I found a cold spot. I tried to follow it to its source. I was moving down the hall and when I got a few yards from the end, something passed across the intersecting corridor ahead of me. It looked like a girl, wearing a long black dress. I rounded the corner, but there was no one there, and there was nowhere she could have gone. The air was freezing. My thermal gauge dropped ten degrees and I noticed the smell of perfume in the air. It was the same sickly-sweet fragrance we smelled before. I made a quick check of the rooms on either side of the hall, but they were all empty."

"What did she look like?" Sandra asked.

"I didn't really get a good look at her face. To tell you the truth, she scared the hell out of me. My heart's still pounding. She looked to be about fifteen or sixteen. Black hair, black dress. She looked solid—like a regular person. But regular people don't just vanish into thin air, do they?"

"Show me where this happened," she said.

They began to walk down the corridor and as they did, I realized that in all the excitement Sandra had left her cassette recorder in the library. Without thinking, I turned and ran down the stairs as fast as I could, then sprinted to the library to fetch the recorder. As I entered the room, I noticed that the candelabra, which had been burning brightly only a few minutes ago, was now extinguished. The strange sight struck me as curious, but I didn't hesitate to ponder its significance. I grabbed the tape recorder and hurried back toward the second floor.

As I began to ascend the main staircase in the entrance hall, an icy chill passed through me, and I was suddenly overcome with an unexplainable feeling of sorrow. The dismal sensation was so overwhelming that my legs nearly buckled beneath me. As I tried to regain my composure I heard whispering from somewhere behind me. Although I knew that there was no one else in the room, I realized I wasn't alone.

The entrance hall fell silent once more, then I heard a voice that seemed to whisper my name. I should have ignored it, dismissing what I heard as the sound of wind whistling through a broken window. I should have continued up the stairs without hesitation and quickly returned to the sanctity of my group. Had I only done so, I might have avoided the grim repercussions of my reckless actions. But I did not. Instead I slowly turned to face whoever or whatever had spoken my name, and in that moment, my lifelong beliefs were shattered.

A tall man, dressed entirely in black, wearing a Victorian-style top hat and coat, was standing on the staircase directly behind me. His dark form wavered like black smoke and his cloak tapered to shadows, fading from sight before reaching the ground. I realized that what I was seeing was no living person, and I knew I could no longer deny the existence of ghosts or the paranormal. Facing the macabre reality that stood before me, I suddenly felt the icy grip of fear taking hold of my heart.

The shadow man whispered my name again, then lifted his head to reveal his ghastly face. I stared in horror as my gaze fell upon two gaping black holes, bored into the center of his head where his eyes should have been. He raised his withered hand toward me and I screamed and stumbled back upon the stairs. I reached out to try to break my fall and as I landed, a jolting pain shot through my shoulder. The pain temporarily took my mind off of the apparition. I looked up, hoping to see nothing more than an empty room, but to my horror, the ghoulish specter was hovering over me, its empty eye sockets blankly staring downward.

The phantom leaned close and its hollow voice hissed, "Leave this place."

Petrified with fear, I began trembling but remained frozen in place. Drawn by my scream, Sandra and Jake ran down the staircase, but came to a dead halt on the landing when they saw the sinister apparition looming over me.

"Get away from her!" Jake shouted, taking a step closer.

The shadow man turned his head in their direction, then slowly began to ascend the steps toward them. Although the apparition's feet were not visible, the wooden stairs sagged and creaked beneath each step he took.

"Get out," he commanded, his raspy voice sounding like the voice of Death itself. The specter moved past Jake, paying him no heed, and proceeded to the landing, stopping to stand before Sandra. Towering over her, the dark phantom lowered his lips to Sandra's ear then he whispered something that I could not hear.

His grim message delivered, the shadow man slowly began to dissolve into a dark mist that wavered in the air, then disappeared completely.

Ron was standing at the top of the staircase, holding his camera in his hands. "What the hell was that thing?"

Sandra looked out over the entry hall, surveying it for vestiges of the grim apparition, and said, "I think it was the ghost of Damon Darklore." She turned to Ronnie. "Did you get a picture of it?"

"Yeah, I think so—right as he was fading away. If it turns out, it'll be fantastic."

Jake gently helped me to my feet and checked my injuries. "Her shoulder's dislocated, and I think her arm might be broken. She needs to get to the hospital."

"So what do we do now?" Ron asked nervously.

Sandra didn't answer. She seemed to be weighing all the crucial factors against one another.

Jake took the opportunity to voice his assessment of our situation. "I've never run from a fight in my life, but this is different. You can't fight something that's not alive. If this thing doesn't want us here, I say we oblige it."

"I agree," Ron said, "I vote we leave. We got what we came for."

Sandra turned to me and I could see a genuine look of concern in her eyes.

"Please Sandra," I pleaded, "let's go home."

Sandra remained quiet for a long moment, then she said, "All my life I've been searching for evidence of life beyond the mortal realm and undeniable proof of its existence. Now I found it... and the truth is more terrifying than I could have ever imagined. I guess you should be careful what you wish for."

She reached into her coat pocket and withdrew the key to the front door. "Let's get the hell out of this damned place."

Just hearing her say that we were leaving made me feel as though a crushing weight had been lifted off of me.

Sandra descended the staircase to where Jake and I stood. "I'll take Pam to the hospital. You guys pack up and meet us there."

"No problem, boss," Jake said, content with her decision.

As we walked toward the front door I glanced back to watch Jake and Ron head back through the south archway and disappear into the engulfing shadows.

I remember only bits and pieces of traveling to the hospital. I must have been in shock, partially from the pain and partially from what my mind could not process. I vaguely remember leaving the mansion and speaking to the sheriff outside the entrance gates. I remember him escorting us to the hospital, but somewhere along the way, I must've blacked out. When I regained consciousness, I was sitting in the emergency room.

Sandra was sitting next to me, watching over me like a mother hen. "Welcome back," she said. "How do you feel?"

"A little groggy, but not so bad. They must've given me something for the pain. I don't remember much." I glanced down to see that my right arm was in a sling and my wrist was wrapped tightly with cloth bandages.

"You dislocated your shoulder and sprained your wrist, but the doctor patched you up, good as new. He said you'll be back to normal in a couple of weeks."

"I'm sorry, Sandra. I messed up."

"That's okay, Pammy. I'm glad to be out of there. We've got enough for our story. Weiss isn't going to be happy that we cut our investigation short, but I wasn't going to risk anyone else's safety." She checked her watch and looked up and down the hospital hallway. "I'm a little worried about Ron and Jake, though. They were supposed to grab the gear and meet us here. They should've been here over an hour ago."

A few minutes later Sheriff Hill entered the hospital lobby.

Sandra walked over to him and handed him the key to the mansion's front door. "I forgot to give this back to you," she said, offering him a halfhearted smile.

The sheriff's eyes conveyed a look of unease as he took the key from her.

"What's wrong?" she asked.

"I need to talk to you, about your two friends." His voice carried a solemn tone. "My deputy said that when they left, they still seemed pretty shook up from whatever happened inside the manor."

"Where are they?" Sandra asked reluctantly, as if she feared hearing his answer.

"Mr. Cooke was driving. He must've lost control of his vehicle in the rain."

"Are they all right?"

"His van ran off the road. They went over the cliff at Widow's Point and crashed into the ocean." He put his hand on her arm. "I'm sorry to have to tell you this, Miss Faraday... but your friends are dead."

Sandra's expression was a garish mixture of devastation and disbelief. Without uttering a word, she staggered to a row of seats near the lobby window and slumped into a chair. The sheriff spoke to her for another ten minutes trying to console her, but she didn't seem to hear a word he said. She just sat there, blankly staring out the window into the rainy night.

I took a seat beside her and closed my eyes, hoping that when I opened them, I would awaken from the nightmare of the past several hours. After a while I dozed off. When I awoke, the first rays of dawn were breaking through the cloud-laden sky. Sandra was no longer sitting in the chair beside me. I scanned the lobby, but she was nowhere to be found.

Sheriff Hill was talking to one of the nurses at the front desk.

When he saw that I was awake, he came straight over to me. "Have you seen Sandra?" I asked.

"The receptionist said that she left the hospital about ten minutes ago."

"What? Why would she leave me here?" I asked. "I'm worried that she might do something crazy."

We went outside and I scoured the parking lot, but her car wasn't there. As I stood there pondering the strange turn of events, the sheriff pulled up in his patrol vehicle.

He opened the passenger door and said, "Get in. I know where she's headed."

I realized that there was only one place he could have meant, and although my closest friend was missing, the thought of returning to Darklore Manor made me hesitate with fear before joining the search to find her. After a brief moment of indecision, I gathered my courage and got in the car.

As we drove to the mansion, I reflected upon all that had transpired in the past day. None of it seemed real. Twenty-four hours ago, the world was a different place. Oblivious to the horrors that dwell in the shadows, I had enjoyed the blissful ignorance shared by rational society. Now, the grim reality of my situation chilled me to the bone, and I realized that from this day forward, my life would never be the same.

We pulled down the forsaken brick road that led to the manor and saw Sandra's car parked beside the front gates. The mansion was veiled by a light mist that obscured its sinister details, but just being on its accursed grounds filled my heart with uncontrollable anxiety. I stayed in the car as the sheriff parked and got out.

Sandra was standing before the locked iron gates, looking toward the manor. Her streaked mascara betrayed the fact that she had been crying. The sheriff approached her slowly.

Without taking her eyes off the mansion, Sandra said, "You can chalk up two more victims to the Darklore curse, Sheriff. It's real and it won't end until the spirits that haunt these grounds are put to rest once and for all. How many more people have to die before you do something about this place?"

"I'll make sure no one goes back inside," he said. "You made it out of there in one piece. You're safe. Go home." He rested a gentle hand on her shoulder. "It's over now."

"No, Sheriff," Sandra whispered, "this is only the beginning."

The investigation was closed, and although things had gone from bad to worse at the mansion, the events that followed were absolutely disastrous for Sandra's career. She reluctantly wrote the article, which was published in *Haunted Havens*, but only after some creative editing by Carl Weiss.

The day that the magazine hit the newsstands I met Sandra for lunch at a local diner. As I entered the restaurant I saw her sitting at a booth in the far corner, scowling and shaking her head in dismay as she read over the article. I slid into the seat across from her, and before I could say hello, she began to voice her disgust.

"That bastard Weiss, he twisted my words. I turned over my

notes and the next thing I know, he's written his own article." She held up the magazine so that I could read the headline, *Haunted House Spooks Investigators.*

My heart sank. "How bad is it?"

Sandra tossed the magazine down onto the table, saying, "See for yourself."

I picked it up and began to read the misleading account, hoping in vain to find something that could be interpreted as positive. The article covered the basic facts but put a pessimistic spin on everything that had transpired. It stated that Sandra investigated Darklore Manor with a team of professional ghost-hunters and "alleged" to have detected the presence of several paranormal entities. It went on to say that she "claimed" to make contact and speak with the spirit of Belladonna Darklore, who told her that she and her family were murdered and that their bodies remain hidden within the walls of Darklore Manor. Although it stated that a thorough search of the home revealed no trace of any human remains, it also mentioned that we discovered a secret doorway in the library but were unable to open it.

Our entire investigation had been reduced to a few paragraphs that glossed over the facts with general statements like "Members of the investigative team reported being overwrought with an unexplainable feeling of sorrow while inside the house," and "Among their numerous claims of paranormal activity they reported hearing a music box playing an eerie melody and allegedly detected a mysterious aroma of lavender on more than one occasion."

One of the final paragraphs described my encounter with the shadow man, casting me as a hapless crybaby who caused the team's early departure and ultimate failure.

My voice filled with anger as I read the paragraph aloud. "'Faraday's visit was cut short after her assistant Pamela Moore was traumatized by a dark entity that appeared on the main staircase. Miss Moore claimed that she was startled as she was ascending the stairs when an icy-cold chill passed through her. She turned to see a man dressed entirely in black, wearing a Victorian-style top hat and coat, standing directly behind her on the stair. Moore was visibly shaken by the encounter and refused to stay in the house. Though photographers shot several rolls of film inside the mansion, none of the pictures could be developed.'"

"Can't we sue him or something?" I asked.

"I'm afraid not," Sandra said. "Weiss made sure that his ass was covered. The contract I signed gave him the right to edit the article at his discretion. Not only did he make us look like amateurs, he didn't mention Ron or Jake by name and removed any allusion to the fact that their deaths might be related to the Darklore curse. I thought he'd make a big deal about it, but instead he made every attempt to distance himself from any controversy. I guess he figured that since he sent them into the house with undeniable knowledge of the curse, he might be liable for a lawsuit blaming him for their wrongful deaths."

Sandra vowed to set the record straight, but before she could even begin her uphill battle, her spirit was crushed beneath an avalanche of devastating events. She wrote a new article and tried to explain the true details of our investigation, but without any evidence to verify the facts, people scoffed at her claims. This started a chain reaction. Once her reputation had been sullied, she couldn't get anyone to publish her work. This caused her to lapse into a deep depression, wherein she stopped writing altogether until eventually her book deal fell through.

Over the next several weeks Sandra became despondent and we grew more and more distant. A few months later, I returned to Pennsylvania and got a low-profile job editing copy for a local newspaper. I tried not to think about the horrible events of the past, hoping to lay them to rest and get on with my life, but the memories of Darklore Manor lingered to haunt me, and no matter how hard I tried, I could not escape its relentless shadow.

The Darklore curse reached its zenith in 1968 when three area teens were reported missing after setting out to spend Halloween night inside the abandoned mansion. Seventeen-year-old Eric Shipley, along with sixteen-year-old James Murphy and Andrea Mather vanished overnight and were never seen again.

Police investigated the unexplained disappearances but found nothing to validate the claims that the three had entered Darklore Manor. On November 9th, 1968, the following article appeared in the Salem Gazette:

> **LOCAL TEENS STILL MISSING**
> Parents of the three Essex Township teenagers who have been missing since October 31st report that they still have hope that their children will be found safe and unharmed. In statements given to the police, friends of the missing teens reported that the three Ipswich High School seniors had plans to hold a séance on Halloween night in Darklore Manor, the deserted mansion along Old Salem Road.
>
> This once-stately Victorian manor has stood unoccupied for the last twenty-seven years and has since fallen into a decrepit state of disrepair. The mansion has been the sight of several unexplained occurrences since the mysterious disappearance of its last owner, Damon Darklore, who vanished in 1941 along with his wife and daughter.
>
> Sheriff George Hill and his deputies have investigated the mansion and reported no noticeable signs of forced entry. "There's something very wrong about that place," stated Hill, "you can actually feel it. Something's just not right. I wish the city would just tear it down and be rid of it, once and for all."

# LOCAL TEENS STILL MISSING

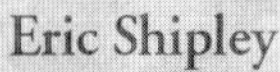
Eric Shipley

Andrea Mather

James Murphy

---

Parents of the three Essex Township teenagers who have been missing since October 31st report that they still have hope that their children will be found safe and unharmed. In statements given to the police, friends of the missing teens reported that the three Ipswich High School seniors had plans to hold a séance on Halloween night in Darklore Manor, the deserted mansion along Old Salem Road.

This once-stately Victorian manor has stood unoccupied for the last twenty-seven years and has since fallen into a decrepit state of disrepair. The mansion has been the sight of several unexplained occurences since the mysterious disappearance of its last owner, Damon Darklore, who vanished in 1941 along with his wife and daughter.

Sheriff George Hill and his deputies have investigated the mansion and reported no noticeable signs of forced entry. "There's something very wrong about that place," stated Hill, "you can actually feel it. Something's just not right. I wish the city would just tear it down and be rid of it, once and for all."

Those with any information as to the teen's whereabouts are asked to call the Essex Co. Sheriff's Dept.

Despite Sheriff Hill's statement, the popular belief was that the teens somehow gained access to the mansion and once inside, the three held a séance to speak with the dead. But according to the rumors things went horribly wrong, and instead of merely communing with spirits, they disturbed and awakened some unnatural force that trapped them within the house and eventually caused their deaths.

Three more years passed before fate drew me back to the unhallowed halls of Darklore Manor. During that time, I researched numerous ancient legends in my quest to shed light on the darkest crevices of the realm of the supernatural. I became well-versed in the mythologies of the world and sought out every bit of information I could find on the various theories of the afterlife. While I spent my days trying to find answers to explain what I had encountered during our tragic expedition, I dreaded falling asleep for fear of the horrific visions that awaited me each night in my dreams. My slumber was haunted by disturbingly vivid nightmares of being trapped inside Darklore Manor with ghastly specters of the dead. Though they were only dreams, they filled my heart with unimaginable terror and I awoke each day thankful to find myself safe in my own bed.

In October of 1971, I received a phone call that changed my nightmares to reality once again.

"I need to talk to you, Miss Moore." The young man's voice conveyed a sense of urgency as he spoke. "It's very important, to you and Miss Faraday."

"Who is this?" I asked. "What do you want?"

"I'd rather explain it in person. I just want a moment of your time. Please, Miss Moore, I need your help." There was a desperate sincerity to the caller's voice that made me want to trust him and help him. Intrigued by his mysterious request, I agreed to meet him at a coffee shop near my work.

As I sat and waited in the crowded cafe, I was caught off-guard by the person that approached me. He was much younger than I expected, looking to be only sixteen or seventeen years old. He was tall and slender with sad brown eyes that matched the color of his shaggy hair. He offered a timid smile, then took a seat opposite me. The wrinkled condition of his faded jeans and flannel shirt made me think that he had slept in his clothes.

"Thank you for coming, Miss Moore."

"So what's this about?" I asked, even more curious than before.

"It's about the house... the one in Gloucester... the one you've been dreaming about."

"What?" I exclaimed, trying to conceal my alarm over the fact that he somehow knew about my dreams.

"I have them too—the horrible dreams about that place. They're not just nightmares, though, are they?" His eyes glanced downward and he stared blankly into a cup of coffee that he clutched between his nervous, pale hands. "There's something inside them that calls to you. Once it gets your scent, it latches onto you and never lets go."

"Who are you?" I asked.

"My name is Theo. Theo Thompson."

As I struggled to remember why his name sounded familiar, his next sentence brought things to light.

"My parents were victims of the Darklore curse. They died right outside the mansion gates ten years ago."

"Yes, I remember reading about the accident."

"It wasn't an accident," Theo said heatedly. "Something deliberately caused my father to crash his car that night. I grew up in Gloucester, and I know all about the ghosts that haunt the manor. I've read all the stories and heard all the rumors that circulate in the local gossip. I pay close attention to what people say, especially when they start to whisper in private. I know all the horrific secrets that have been swept under the rug since the Darklore curse claimed its first victim."

"So what made you decide to contact me?"

"You know that story about the teenagers who disappeared near Gloucester three years ago?"

"Yes. They were supposed to have been inside Darklore Manor."

"That's right," he confirmed. "They were my friends. It's my fault they're dead."

"What makes you think that they're dead? The paper only said they were missing and as far as I know, no bodies have ever been found. They could still turn up."

"No, they won't. I know because I saw them go into that house, but they never came back out. The police searched the place but didn't find any trace of them. That means they're still in there... and they're not alive."

"What do you think happened to them?"

Theo sat back in his seat and took a deep breath. "My grandfather belonged to the Knights of Thule, so did my father. After my parents died I found an old brass key hidden among my father's personal belongings. I never saw anything like it. It was the key that was given to him when he became a member of the Knights of Thule."

My curiosity was piqued. "So what's this got to do with your missing friends?"

"They wanted to hold a séance in Darklore Manor on Halloween night. It was a dare. I told them about the key I had. They knew a way to get into the house through an unlocked window. I was afraid to go inside. I gave them the key, then chickened out. I'm responsible for whatever happened to them inside that house, and in a way, Miss Moore, so are you."

"How am I responsible?"

"The magazine article about your investigation inside Darklore Manor mentioned the secret door you discovered in the library—the one with the strange keyhole."

As he spoke, a grim realization began to sweep over me.

"I gave them the key," he said solemnly, "but you told them where to use it."

My stomach began to twist in knots as the full weight of Theo's words set in. I was unable to respond to his accusation.

"The nightmares we have... it's them," he said, "they're haunting us, and it won't ever stop until we find their bodies and set their souls free."

"No, Theo, it's not your friends that haunt your dreams. It may look like them and sound like them, but it's something else. Something's been in that house for a long time. It may have existed deep in the earth below Darklore Manor for centuries before the mansion was ever built. I've done some research on the history of the area and I found some startling legends dating back hundreds of years. According to Indian lore, the area was the resting place of an ancient spirit that had the power to command the shadows. The surrounding woodlands were shunned by the regional tribes who believed that the forests harbored dark spirits that hunted men."

"I don't doubt that the stories are true, but it doesn't change the fact that my friends are dead and their spirits are trapped inside Darklore Manor."

"There's nothing we can do."

"Just ignoring the problem isn't going to make it go away or help us sleep at night. We have to do something to set things right."

"So what's your plan?"

"I'm going inside the manor and I need your help."

"I... I can't..." I stammered. "I can't go back there. I'm sorry."

"That's okay. I didn't really expect you to, but I need you to convince Miss Faraday to come back with me. If she can make contact with them, maybe we can put their spirits to rest. I can't get in touch with her, though."

"That doesn't surprise me. She doesn't talk to anyone anymore. We haven't spoken in years."

"Please, Miss Moore—if you ever want your life to be normal again, please help me."

"All right, Theo. I'll see what I can do."

It came as no surprise to discover that Theo had hitchhiked all the way from Gloucester to plead his case with me. I agreed to give him a lift back to New York and introduce him to Sandra, but I made it clear that after that, he was on his own. He was hoping that Sandra would drive him back to Gloucester if he could convince her to return to Darklore Manor.

Our first task was locating Sandra. In an attempt to sever all ties to her past, she had moved from her old residence and left no forwarding address. After hitting a dead end with all my old contact information, I made a phone call to Sandra's mother who was more than happy to provide me with her daughter's new address. Sandra had purchased a bungalow in a secluded area of wooded countryside in upper New York State. The remote setting was a drastically diverse change from her town house in the city, but it was a perfect location for someone who wanted to shut herself off from the rest of the world.

We arrived at her home late in the afternoon. I told Theo to wait in the car while I went inside and broke the ice for him. Sandra didn't seem surprised to see me when she opened the door, but I was somewhat unprepared for the startling change in her appearance. Her sandy blonde hair had turned completely white and her face and figure looked extremely gaunt, as if she had been slowly withering away for the last four years. I tried to conceal my shock at her appearance as she invited me inside, but it was no use attempting to hide my feelings from her.

The interior of her house was cluttered with religious artifacts from every known culture on Earth. The walls were covered with mystical symbols, crosses, sacred talismans and holy wards, while incense and votives burned before pagan statues that adorned ritual shrines of protection. She was apparently trying to create a spiritual buffer zone to keep something at bay.

Ignoring the obvious questions about her home and appearance, I began the conversation with some innocent small-talk. "So how have you been?" I asked.

"I'm fine," Sandra replied, flashing an unconvincing grin, "I've been doing some work in the private sector. I have some very influential clients." She picked up an open bottle of wine from her kitchen counter and asked, "Can I pour you a glass?"

"No, thank you."

"Suit yourself," she said, then emptied the remainder of the wine into a crystal goblet and gulped it down.

"I thought you had a rule about drinking alone."

"Rules were made to be broken. I was just drowning some old memories."

I picked up a half-empty bottle of sleeping pills from the kitchen table. "Having trouble sleeping?" I asked.

"No," Sandra laughed, "I take those once in a while to help me relax. Like I said, I'm fine."

"Don't lie to me, Sandra. I've known you long enough to be able to tell when you're not being honest."

"I don't know what you're talking about."

I decided to get straight to the point. "I know that you're still having the dreams about Darklore Manor. I'm having them too, and we're not the only ones."

Sandra dropped her stoic facade and her expression changed to one of serious concern.

"Why did you come here, Pam?"

"You know about the three teenagers who disappeared in the mansion, right?"

Sandra didn't respond.

"They went in there because they read the article about our investigation. They tried to make contact with the ghosts that haunt the manor, but now I think their souls are trapped in there. I've been contacted by one of their friends who thinks that you might be able to help."

"Nothing can help them now," she said coldly.

"Why?"

"Because I know what happened to them inside that house."

I stared at her incredulously. The certainty in her voice was unnerving. "How do you know?"

"I saw it... I saw it in my dreams." She stared into the bottom of her empty goblet as if it were some sort of crystal ball. "I couldn't tell anybody. Even if anyone actually believed me, there would have been another investigation. More people would have gone into that hellhole and more people would have died. I won't have any more deaths on my conscience."

"The dreams aren't real," I retorted. "They're not psychic visions, they're just nightmares. Like I said, I'm having them too."

Sandra shook her head. "No, Pam. Trust me, if you had seen the things that I've seen, we wouldn't be having this conversation."

Sandra stepped into the living room and lit a fresh votive candle to replace one that had burned down. "In my dreams, it's as if I'm there again, inside Darklore Manor. The sights, the sounds—everything seems so real. I've been keeping a chronicle of them." She opened an antique cabinet and ran her fingers over a large rack of cassette tapes marked with various dates and pulled out a tape labeled 10-31-68. "This one ought to interest you." She placed the tape into a cassette player, then pressed the play button.

"It begins in the library." Sandra's recorded voice sounded hoarse as she began her deposition. "The central bookcase creaks away from the wall and the secret door opens to reveal a narrow stone staircase leading down into darkness. A hidden chamber deep below the manor conceals long-buried secrets of arcane rites. Ancient tomes and tattered scrolls hold forbidden rituals of black magic. Strange inscriptions cover the stone walls and mark the final resting place of those lost and forgotten. Skeletal remains line the walls of the ancestral vault, a grim testament to those who did not escape this living nightmare. A sinister confession from long ago reveals that there is no rest for the wicked.

"Sacred candles burn as a beacon, summoning restless souls to the séance. That which has lain dormant for so many years has been awakened from its deathly slumber. Beyond the midnight hour, dread things arise from the shadowy depths. Buried and forgotten long ago, darkness immortal has been unleashed. Ancient incantations echo throughout the forsaken crypt. Resurrected from the grave, it hungers for life once more.

"There will be no returning on this night. Nothing will ever escape these walls again."

After a moment of silence, Sandra pressed the stop button.

"This doesn't prove anything," I said, "but it's made me see things clearly. The last thing I ever wanted to do was go back inside that house, but seeing you this way made me realize that I'd rather face my fears than end up like this." I gestured to the surrounding shrines that stood as monuments to Sandra's fear and paranoia.

"We left part of ourselves in that house," I said, "and whatever is in that place has latched onto us. It's been wearing us down like a wolf stalking wounded prey. I don't want to spend the rest of my life like a frightened little rabbit hiding in its hole." I was surprised by the intensity of the anger in my voice. "We're not living, Sandra, we're just existing. I want my life back and if it means risking my neck, then so be it. We need to go back."

A look of terror swept across Sandra's face. "I'm not going anywhere. We were lucky to make it out of there the first time. If you go back, you're risking more than your life." Sandra's voice grew louder. "Now it's awake, and it's loose inside that house. It's much stronger than it was before, but it's still hungry. It won't be denied this time, and it won't ever let you go."

"I have to do something!" I shouted. "I can't live like this. I don't want to be haunted by this thing anymore."

"Do you really want to know what happened to those kids that night? Do you want to hear all the horrific details of everything they encountered in their final hours? Because if you're actually considering going back in there, I think you should know exactly what will be waiting for you."

My eyes welled with tears as I turned to leave. "Goodbye, Sandra."

"They snuck into the house through a window," Sandra whispered. "There were three of them—dressed in black from head to toe. Andrea Mather, James Murphy and Eric Shipley. They brought flashlights and candles to light their way, just like we did. But they had something we didn't. They had the key to the door in the library."

I stopped in my tracks and turned back to face her as she continued her tale.

"They made their way through the cobwebbed halls into the library. Andrea placed the key in the lock and twisted it, then James pulled the heavy bronze door open. Without hesitating to consider the consequences of their actions, they foolishly descended the winding staircase into the dank regions far beneath the mansion.

"The trio emerged in a large circular vault that held a macabre treasury of arcane relics. As they scanned the chamber with their flashlights they began to distinguish strange inscriptions covering the walls, and the skulls of humans and animals slowly emerged from the surrounding shadows. A weathered stone altar and pedestal inscribed with runic designs stood in the center of the room. Andrea stepped closer to examine a worm-eaten book of ancient spells, which sat open upon the pedestal. Beside the decayed tome, a large ceremonial dagger rested alongside a smaller blade that looked like an ornate straight razor.

"On the wall opposite the entrance, a wide stone corridor led further into the darkness. James and Eric boldly set forth to explore the tunnel but found that after a short distance the passage ended abruptly at a door of solid granite. An inscription above the doorway marked the sealed chamber as the Darklore burial vault. They strained against the heavy stone slab in an attempt to gain access to the crypt, but their best combined efforts had no effect on the impenetrable door. Realizing that they could go no further, they returned to the main chamber where they had left their friend.

"Andrea lit several candles and placed them around the room, illuminating the gloomy vault in a dim yellow glow. The boys watched as she drew a large circle on the dusty stone floor, then traced a triangle inside it. She quickly surrounded the design with mystical symbols, copying a diagram from an old piece of parchment she had brought with her. When she was done, she set three black candles around the circle at the points of the triangle. The three teens sat on the floor around the ritual circle and joined hands as Andrea invoked the spirit of Belladonna Darklore.

"As she spoke, subtle whispers echoed from the surrounding shadows, as if in response to her commands, and a swirling mist began to materialize in the center of the circle. The three sat speechless as the mist began to expand and take the form of a woman shrouded entirely in black. The dark apparition hovered above them for a moment, then slowly drifted down the corridor that led to the Darklore crypt, vanishing into the shadows that concealed the tomb door. The sound of stone grinding against stone issued forth from the darkness, and then the air grew deathly cold as low laughter echoed from the tunnel. The candles grew dim and expired one by one as if some unseen hand were deliberately extinguishing them.

"The trio sprang to their feet and hastened to leave the unhallowed underworld of Darklore Manor. Their flashlights spared them from being trapped in total darkness as they searched for the staircase that led back to the surface. They stumbled toward the exit, but stopped in their tracks when they realized they were not alone in the chamber.

"A small figure loomed before them. It stood on the narrow staircase, blocking their way. An eerie halo of writhing shadows encircled its petite form and its red eyes glistened like blazing rubies in the darkness. It was the doll.

"Eric cautiously extended a trembling hand toward the porcelain figure. He picked the doll up to examine it closely, and as he did, the sinister toy twisted in his grip, opening its mouth wide. He screamed in terror as the doll dug its tiny teeth into his palm, biting down hard and drawing a stream of blood from his flesh. Eric shook his arm violently, sending the doll careening into the shadows across the chamber. Andrea and James tried to run for the stairs, but before they could make their escape, the surrounding shadows seemed to come alive. Spectral forms made of black mist rose from the spot where Eric's blood had spilled.

"A tall shadow lashed out toward Eric, hitting him in the chest, thrusting him backward and knocking him off his feet. A claw-like hand emerged from the spectral mist and crept across the bloodstained floor toward the dazed boy. Before he could get up, long black fingers ending in sharp talons grabbed him by the jaw and held his head against the floor. He struggled in vain against the phantom arm that pinned him to the ground. The ghostly hand twisted his head to the left, and he watched in horror as a small figure stepped out of the shadows. His eyes widened as they met the burning gaze of the sinister doll once more. The living toy jerked toward him, clutching the straight razor in its hands. He kicked and struggled as the porcelain figure advanced closer and closer toward his face. The doll's tiny lips drew back to expose its bloodstained teeth, forming a wicked grin upon the crackled porcelain. He screamed for help as the gleaming blade descended upon him again and again.

"James tried to help his friend, but the shadows rose to engulf him. The black mist encircled him, ensnaring him in its sinister grasp. The smoky coils twisted around him, constricting their grip. It lifted him off the ground, squeezing the breath out of his lungs and crushing his ribcage. His eyes bulged with terror as the sickening sound of cracking bones echoed off the walls of the stone chamber.

"Andrea retreated into the furthest reaches of the crypt, stumbling through the darkness in her attempt to escape the nightmare that was unfolding around her. Soon her friend's shrieks ended, leaving her alone in the tomb's unnerving silence. Her quivering hands fumbled to light a match and when her eyes adjusted to the meager flickering light she found herself inside the Darklore family tomb. The heavy stone slab that sealed the chamber had somehow been cast aside and she had blindly entered the deepest reaches of the crypt.

"In the flame's dim glow, she could see the skeletal remains of three bodies. The withered form of a woman in a tattered black gown rested on a marble slab in the center of the room and two other decayed corpses lay on the floor. Andrea crept toward the skeletal figure that lay in a deathly repose upon the black marble altar, realizing that the desiccated corpse could be none other than Belladonna Darklore. As she neared the body, her match burned down, extinguishing her lone source of light and as she nervously hastened to strike a new match, an unsettling noise echoed from somewhere within the confines of the pitch black tomb. The sound of whispered laughter emanated from the shadows, chilling her to the bone. Andrea quickly lit another match then froze in place in front of the empty altar. Staggering backward, she gasped in horror and turned to face the cadaverous form of Belladonna which now stood between her and the only exit. A horrible smile formed on the corpse's withered lips as she brandished the sacrificial dagger from the ritual pedestal, raising it in front of her rotting face. Andrea screamed and recoiled in terror, dropping her match to the floor. The flame expired, plunging her into the consuming blackness of the crypt amidst a torrent of bloodcurdling shrieks. Then the tomb fell silent once more."

When Sandra finished her tale, she turned to face me. "There you have it," she said, "believe it or not."

Her horrific story was incredible, but I believed every word. As I stared deep into her hollow eyes I reflected upon my past and came to a stark revelation. My life to this point had been a series of conditioned responses. Whenever I felt threatened, I had always run away to hide from my fears. But now I was tired of running. It was time to take a stand. And even though I understood the full extent of the horrors that dwelled within the manor, I was determined to return and confront them.

"I'm not the same person I was four years ago," I said. "I've learned a thing or two about exorcising demons, whether real or imagined."

"I see," Sandra said, sighing heavily. "I wish I could help you."

"Maybe you can. I've been curious about something for a long time now."

"What's that?"

"The day we were inside the mansion, when we encountered the spirit of Damon Darklore on the staircase, he whispered something to you. What did he say?"

Sandra closed her eyes, trying to recall the exact words. "He said 'Dust and shadows cannot die,' then he whispered, 'More blood must be spilled.'" Her voice trembled as she repeated the ominous message.

Without fully comprehending the meaning of the cryptic words, I committed them to memory for the bleak mission that lay ahead of me. Before I left, Sandra gave me a tearful hug and repeated how sorry she was for everything that had happened. As I walked out the door, I realized that I would probably never see her again.

The trip back to Gloucester was strangely enlightening. Along the way, Theo shared a wide range of conspiracy theories regarding the manor, the Darklore family, the Knights of Thule and the good citizens of his home town. He also reminisced about his three friends. He told me that Eric wanted to be an actor and James loved sports. I couldn't bring myself to tell him about Sandra's vision of what happened to them inside the mansion.

"Andrea was more into it than the others," he said. "She told everyone that she was a descendant of Cotton Mather, the witch who was hung during the Salem trials. She read a lot of books on black magic and the occult. We saw an old photograph of

Belladonna Darklore once and told her that she looked like her."

As Theo continued to talk, I pretended to listen, but my mind wandered to thoughts of how this all tied into what Sandra had told me. Somehow, everything seemed to center around Belladonna, but I couldn't piece it together.

"I'm curious, Theo. Why didn't you ever go to the police?"

Theo gazed out of the car window, his face stony and somehow older than his years. "I don't trust them. They're part of the conspiracy. They've been covering up the truth for years."

"When Pamela and I were in Gloucester, Sheriff Hill seemed genuinely concerned about..."

"Don't let him fool you," Theo interrupted. "He's the worst one."

"Why do you say that?"

"He's the one who found Councilman Franklin's body hanging in the manor. Rumor has it that Franklin left a suicide note that said, 'Forgive me for my sins,' or something like that, but the official report says that there wasn't any note. The sheriff's hiding something."

Though he had a long list of suspicions about everyone in Gloucester, Theo remained focused on his mission. He missed his friends and his parents. Everyone that he ever held dear had been taken by Darklore Manor and the ghosts that haunted it, and he wanted revenge.

We arrived in Gloucester early Halloween evening, just after the sun had set. The leering faces of jack-o-lanterns watched from the shadows, welcoming us with fiendish smiles as we drove into town. Piles of red and brown fallen leaves lined the streets and sidewalks beneath barren trees that stretched skyward toward the crescent moon. The town itself looked exactly the same as I remembered it. Nothing had changed. It was if it had been frozen in time for the past decade.

As we headed out along Old Salem Road a heavy fog had begun to roll in from the seacoast. Before long we were engulfed in a dense mist. When we got about a quarter mile from the mansion, Theo directed me down a dirt path off the main road.

"The cops will be watching this place tonight," he said. "They do every Halloween now."

We left the car hidden in the trees and Theo led me through the woods. While an eerie calm had settled over the misty forest, the distant screech of owls interrupted the silence at irregular intervals. After a short trek, we emerged from the woods alongside the spiked gate that surrounded the house. I glanced back toward the front of the property. The stone griffons loomed like enormous vultures perched upon the gates, waiting to pick the flesh from the bones of the dead. As I squinted into the fog I could barely make out the outline of a police cruiser, parked off the side of the road, across from the entrance gate.

"See?" Theo whispered, pointing to the car, "what'd I tell ya?" He nodded back in the opposite direction and said, "This way."

I followed him along the wrought iron fence that surrounded the manor till we came to one of the tall stone posts behind the house. A narrow gap between the post and the iron rails allowed us to squeeze through and onto the property. The dense fog obscured the manor house, reducing it to a towering silhouette looming in the distance. As we drew nearer, the sinister architecture of the mansion became visible through the mist, and we beheld Darklore Manor in its awful majesty. Black and silent, heartless and deathly still, this was indeed a house of horrors and I fully dreaded whatever nightmares awaited us within.

We crept up to a window near the back door. Theo withdrew a pocket knife and slid it between the panes. Within seconds he had thrown the window latch.

"Wait here," he said, "I'll unlock the back door."

Quickly and quietly, he slipped inside the house. A few seconds later I heard the sound of the door bolt being thrown. The heavy back door opened and Theo waved me inside. I took a deep breath of the autumn air, then entered the house, locking the door behind me.

We headed straight for the library, trying not to use our flashlights unless absolutely necessary, and then only for a minimal amount of time. We avoided passing near any of the mansion's front windows for fear of alerting the occupants of the patrol car. The echoes of our shuffling footsteps sounded like voices whispering in the surrounding shadows. I kept my eyes focused straight ahead, ignoring the unnatural shapes that seemed to stir and slither in the periphery of my vision.

We made our way through the entrance hall and into the south wing, then down the corridor of portraits into the library. Once we entered the chamber, I closed the library doors and drew the heavy, dusty curtains before lighting a lantern. Cobwebs clung to the monstrous faces of gargoyles in the four corners of the room but their combined scowls could not conjure the sense of menace that was created by the ominous portrait of Edmund Darklore that seemed to watch our every move us as we made our way across the chamber.

When we reached the far end I rested my hand on the central bookshelf. "This is the one."

Theo approached the tall shelf and said, "If we're lucky, the door will be open or the key will still be in the lock." He grabbed hold of the bookcase and pulled it toward him to reveal the tarnished bronze door hidden behind it, but the entrance was sealed shut and there was no key to be found.

"Can you pick the lock?" I asked.

"I don't know. I'll give it a try. The key had a complicated design, so this might not be easy."

He withdrew a set of lock picks from his jacket pocket and inserted two of the tools in the keyhole. After a few minutes, Theo voiced his frustration. "This might take a while. I can shift the tumblers, but..."

"Shhh," I interrupted. "I thought I heard something."

We sat in silence for a moment, listening intently for any telltale noises that might alert us to unseen dangers. I could feel my heartbeat pounding in my chest. My pulse quickened as I heard the sound of floorboards creaking outside the library door.

"Footsteps," I whispered, "and it sounds like their coming closer."

I put out the lantern and we quickly hid behind the drapes that covered the large bay window. We heard the library door slowly squeal open, followed by the sound of footsteps entering the room. I peered out from behind the curtains to catch a glimpse of whoever had followed us into the library and what I saw made me shudder with terror. A tall shadow stood in the doorway, blocking the only exit.

In desperation, I turned back toward the window, searching for a means of escape, but the leaded glass was firmly sealed in place. I looked at Theo and noticed that he was staring at something that had caught his attention outside. In the distance, a dark figure rose from the mist and was slowly moving across the lawn. At first it appeared to be no more than an obscure silhouette amidst the consuming fog, but as the figure drew closer, it became more distinguished and I could discern the form of a young woman, draped entirely in black. Her dark hair floated in the breeze as she slowly drifted along beneath the moonlight, then she vanished into the mist once more.

The sound of footsteps resumed, drawing my attention back to the unknown intruder inside the library as it slowly made its way across the room. The floorboards creaked as the shadow approached to within a few feet of the window then the footsteps stopped and the room fell silent once more. I took a deep breath and held it, daring not to move or utter a sound. Suddenly, an icy chill crept down my spine and some inner sense caused me to look back behind me. I slowly turned my head to face the window and as I did, I was met with a ghastly sight. The shadowy specter that had disappeared in the fog was right outside the window, leering at me through the glass with soulless black eyes, its deathly pale face only a few inches from my own.

I screamed and jumped backward, and as I did, a tall figure threw open the curtains and my eyes were accosted by a blinding light.

"What the hell is going on here?" a deep voice boomed. The intruder lowered his flashlight beam and I stared into the familiar face of Sheriff Hill.

Frantically, I blurted, "There was something outside the window! It was there in the fog—a ghost... a woman dressed in black. I think it was the spirit of Belladonna Darklore." I turned back toward the window, but the ghoulish phantom was gone.

The sheriff squinted as he peered out into the misty night. "There's nothing out there now," he said.

Theo shone his flashlight on the sheriff and asked, "What are you doing here?"

"I should be asking you that question, Theo," the sheriff replied, making it clear that the two were no strangers. Sheriff Hill shifted his stern gaze to me and said, "I got a weird phone call from your friend Sandra earlier this evening. She told me that you'd be coming here tonight. She sounded pretty shook up. She made me promise to look into it. To be honest, you two are the just about the last people I would've ever expected to find inside this place. What on earth could ever have possessed you to come back here?"

After taking a second to compose myself, I calmly answered, "We think we may know what happened to the kids that disappeared three years ago."

"Is that so?"

"They're in there," I said, pointing to the bronze door adorned with the shield and runes. "It leads to a crypt below the mansion."

Sheriff Hill stepped over to the hidden door and tested it to see if it would open, but it didn't budge.

"How would you know where this door leads?" he asked. "And what makes you think that those missing kids are down there?"

I shook my head to concede that I had no good answer. "You wouldn't believe me if I told you."

"Try me."

"Don't waste your breath," Theo said, glaring at the sheriff, "he's not going to help us. He doesn't want anyone to know the truth about what happened here. He and the rest of the city officials are in it together. It's a conspiracy to bury the town's horrible secret."

"That's not true, Theo," the sheriff replied patiently. "I'm not the enemy. Believe it or not, I want to get to the bottom of this just as badly as you do." From his shirt pocket he withdrew a large brass key. "This should lead us to some answers."

Theo's eyes grew wide. "Where did you get that from?"

"It belonged to Richard Franklin. It was inside an envelope that was in his pocket when he killed himself. I did a little digging over the years and I found out that all the members of the Brotherhood had their own keys to the ritual chamber. But you already knew that, didn't you, Theo?"

Theo's expression became less agitated and his tone softened. "I heard rumors that Mr. Franklin left a suicide note, but the facts were covered up."

"It was the mayor's decision," the sheriff said, "and it wasn't a suicide note. It only had two words, written in Franklin's handwriting."

"What did it say?" Theo asked.

"'Forgive me.'"

"For what?" I asked.

"I don't know for sure," he said, "but I have my suspicions."

"Didn't the note say anything else?" Theo asked.

The sheriff cast a stern look in his direction. "There was one other word, but it wasn't in the note. It was carved into his forehead."

"What did it say?"

The sheriff paused as if considering whether or not to reveal the dark secret he had kept for the past decade, then uttered the word: "'Sinner.'"

After a brief moment of contemplation, I said, "According to Sandra, Belladonna's spirit told her that the sinners had to be punished."

"Why would Franklin come back here?" Theo asked.

The sheriff shrugged, looking around at the grim, macabre décor of the library. "No one really knows why he came to the house—maybe to lock the last key inside the vault. He sure as hell didn't come here to hang himself."

"Something summoned him here," I said. "He had to heed its call. There's something in this house—an evil presence that's been here since before the mansion was built. I think it may have been here for centuries. The spirits of everyone who died here are trapped inside this house. Something is keeping their souls from finding eternal rest."

"If you've got a theory, I'd like to hear it," the sheriff said.

I stepped over to the large painting depicting the war between angels and demons, keeping my flashlight trained on it. Radiant seraphim thrust golden lances down upon winged devils, sending them plummeting into the fires of Hell. "As you may know, Lucifer was once an angel who was said to have been transformed into a loathsome demon after he and his legions were driven out of Heaven. Lesser-known tales describe other fallen angels known as the Grigori and the Nephilim, also known as the Watchers, who walked among men as gods, sharing arcane knowledge that had been forbidden to mankind. It was said that these unearthly creatures spawned children with mortal women and instructed their offspring in the ways of dark magic. After they were banished from the kingdom of Heaven, the Watchers were said to reside deep in the earth, seeking the solace of shadows and darkness.

"Similar legends have been recorded in every ancient mythology. The Sumerian texts contained within the Ebon Scrolls describe monstrous deities known as the Dark Gods that were said to rule the Earth eons ago. These entities preyed upon mortal lusts and desires, using men's weaknesses and fears against them.

According to the legends, the Dark Gods fed on the blood and sorrow of humans and captured the souls of their victims."

"I'm not sure I follow you," the sheriff said, his brow furrowing. "Are you saying that this place is haunted by an ancient demon, or do you think it's some sort of fallen angel?"

"I think they're one and the same."

The sheriff pondered my words for a long moment, then said, "I'm not a superstitious person, Miss Moore. I never used to believe the stories about this place being haunted or cursed, but I've seen the evidence and I can't deny the facts. Over the years I've witnessed things that have changed my opinion and I've come to the conclusion that something unnatural resides here. Some people call it evil. I really don't know what it is. Nobody does."

The sheriff walked over to the secret door and slid his key into the lock.

"The way I see it," Sheriff Hill said, glancing back at me with a half smile, "there's only one way to find out." He turned the key and pulled the heavy door toward him. With the groan of rusted hinges, the bronze barrier swung open to reveal a narrow stone staircase leading down into thick, subterranean shadows.

Theo took a step toward the door, but the sheriff stopped him. "Hold on," he said. The sheriff walked over to the medieval weapons display hanging on the wall behind the desk and removed a broadsword. He stepped back to the secret entrance and wedged the blade between the door and the frame, securely propping the entrance open.

"I'm not taking any chances," he said. "No one knows where we are and I don't want to get trapped down there."

Sheriff Hill led the way and Theo and I followed him into the dismal chambers concealed below Darklore Manor. The sour scent of must and mildew filled the air as we descended the winding stairway that twisted deep into the earth. We emerged in a large circular vault that had been quarried from the bedrock far beneath the mansion. The stagnant air was cold and stale, and although there were no apparent signs of life, I could not escape the disturbing feeling that we were not alone in the chamber.

Macabre mementos of unholy rites filled the hidden sanctum, and as I looked over the scene, I realized that everything was just as Sandra had described it. A sacrificial altar adorned with runic symbols stood in the center of the chamber beside a pedestal supporting a massive tome. The horned skull of a goat hung prominently displayed over the front of the ceremonial shrine and three black candles rested on the floor beside the altar, marking the perimeter of Andrea Mather's ritual circle. The fact that the chamber matched Sandra's description seemed to confirm her vision regarding the fate of the missing teens, yet their bodies were nowhere in sight.

An antique table against the outer wall held several relics that rested undisturbed beneath a layer of cobwebs and dust. Theo stepped closer to examine the concealed items and with a quick swipe of his hand he unveiled stacks of crumbling scrolls, occult books, a row of mortuary urns and an old wooden strongbox. He opened the lid of the chest, revealing several tarnished skeleton keys inside.

Theo held one up for us to see, announcing, "These must be the keys from the dead Knights of Thule."

While Theo continued to rummage through the tomes and scrolls, Sheriff Hill surveyed the surrounding walls with his flashlight. The devilish face of a horned greenman relief was chiseled into the dark stone above a Latin inscription that read:

*Facilis descencus Averno.*
*Qui non vetat peccare, cum possit, iubet.*
*Sine cruce, sine luce, nihil interit.*
*Pulvis et umbra sumus.*

As the sheriff studied the engraved words, I began to translate the message aloud.

Facilis descencus Averno.
Qui non vetat peccare, cum
possit, iubet. Sine cruce,

*"The descent to Hell is effortless.
He who does not forbid sin, commands it.
Without the cross, without the light, nothing dies.
We are but dust and shadows."*

"What does it mean?" the sheriff asked.

"I'm not quite sure," I answered hesitantly. "It sounds ominous. Maybe it's a warning... or maybe it's just some esoteric mumbo-jumbo."

The sheriff ran the flashlight beam along the mildewed walls, revealing a dozen human skulls set into niches surrounding the chamber. Upon closer inspection we could see that the word "Sinner" had been crudely carved into the forehead of each of the skulls.

Across the room, another passageway led deeper into the unexplored regions of the crypt. We followed the tunnel to its end where an ornate doorway was carved into the bedrock. The top of the stone door frame was adorned with the effigy of a weeping woman and other fiendish faces were sculpted into the sides of the entrance. The name "Darklore" was chiseled into the granite above the doorway, while the bottom of the doorframe held the inscription "*Ecce Quomodo Moritur.*"

The sheriff squinted at the words, then asked, "What does it say?"

"'Behold the way of death,'" I whispered. "It's the entrance to the Darklore family crypt."

The doorway stood open, like the gaping maw of a ravenous beast. As we crept toward it, strange whispers seemed to echo from somewhere within. After a moment of hesitation, Sheriff Hill crossed the ominous threshold into the yawning tomb with Theo and I close behind him. Once inside, we were immediately assailed by the foul stench of death and decay. I relit my lantern and hung it from an iron sconce set into the stone wall between two arches.

To the left of the entrance, the granite door of the tomb leaned against the wall at a crooked angle, as if it had been violently thrown aside by some enormous force. A strange symbol marked the back of the door in what appeared to be dried blood. The surrounding walls were lined with sealed vaults bearing the graven names of those interred within. Morbid faces of stone peered down from archways above each of the graves, adding to the atmosphere of foreboding and suffering that permeated the oppressive chamber.

The withered corpse of a young woman rested on a black marble altar in the center of the crypt and the skeletal remains of several other bodies lay on the floor.

The sheriff passed his flashlight over the grisly scene, tallying the mutilated corpses. "Six bodies," he muttered. "They're all here—the missing kids and the three members of the Darklore family that disappeared thirty years ago."

Theo breathed a sigh of pain and relief as he recognized the bodies of his lost friends among the dead. "We've got to get them out of here. They won't rest in peace until they receive a proper burial."

Sheriff Hill laid a consoling hand on Theo's shoulder and said, "We will, Theo, but not now. There'll have to be an investigation. We'll get a crew down here to remove the bodies, but we have to figure out what happened to them."

The sheriff turned his attention to the corpse that lay upon the marble slab in the center of the room. Keeping a safe distance from the altar, he shone his flashlight over the body to examine the lifeless form of Belladonna. Her head was thrown back and her mouth gaped open wide as if she had died screaming in agony. The tattered fabric of her black gown hung over the sides of the marble slab and her skeletal hands clutched an ornate dagger that rested upon her chest. A crusty coat of dried blood covered the ceremonial blade in a dark shade of crimson.

None of us said a word as we contemplated the horrific sights that surrounded us in the forsaken crypt. Lost in solemn reflection we stood frozen in the hush that had befallen us until the unnerving silence was broken by a distant sound. A haunting refrain echoed through the outer corridor, and though I had not heard the eerie melody since my fateful first visit to Darklore Manor, I recognized it immediately. It was Belladonna's music box—and the sound was coming closer.

The sheriff aimed his flashlight beam through the doorway and down the gloomy tunnel to reveal an unearthly mist that was steadily creeping toward us. The eerie vapor began to seep into the crypt, filling the chamber with a pale green fog. Theo started to run for the door but stopped in his tracks when he saw that the outer corridor was blocked. A dark figure was slowly advancing down the tunnel, floating through the gossamer mist. As it drew closer we could see that it was a woman, shrouded entirely in black, her ebon hair and gown flowing behind her like a trail of shadows. It was the same dark phantom I had seen outside the library window. It was the undead specter of Belladonna Darklore. Even though her decayed remains lay upon the altar behind us, her restless spirit was eternally cursed to wander the manor and grounds.

The haunting chimes grew louder, and a ghostly, child-like voice joined in the melody. The sickly sweet fragrance of lavender replaced the rancid smell of mildew as the shrouded spirit entered the crypt. Her black eyes glistened in stark contrast to the pallor of her bone-white flesh and her alabaster hands clutched a crimson bundle to her chest. The dark phantom hung suspended in the air just inside the doorway and as the ghostly mist began to settle around her, we could see that she was holding the porcelain doll cradled in her arms.

The sheriff withdrew his revolver and trained it on the apparition, and the doll's head slowly turned to cast a menacing stare in his direction. As Belladonna continued her hypnotic song, her voice had a mesmerizing effect, like the mythical sirens of ancient Greece. My mind began to grow numb and I found myself losing my will to resist. The doll extended its hands in our direction and we watched in horror as the sheriff ambled listlessly toward it, like a slave in thrall to his master's commands. Unable to fight the impulse to comply, he holstered his pistol then reached out to embrace the sinister toy. The doll's lips drew back in a wicked smile, exposing its jagged fangs.

A split second before the sheriff took hold of the diabolic doll, another shape emerged from the mist behind Belladonna. In the blink of an eye, the mysterious figure lashed out violently with a large blade, slicing through Belladonna's ethereal form and slashing the doll in two, severing it in half at the waist. As the remnants of Belladonna's spectral form dissolved into the fog, the doll's torso fell to the ground hissing and screeching.

The shadowy figure stepped into the lantern's light and we gazed upon the face of our mysterious savior with awe and dismay. There in the doorway stood Sandra, clutching a sword in her hand like an avenging angel. As the dismembered doll scampered to crawl away, Sandra stepped on it and held it beneath her boot. She swung the sword downward, delivering one final blow, landing the blade between the doll's burning red eyes and shattering its porcelain head to pieces.

Breathing heavily, she asked, "Is everyone okay?"

"I think so," I whispered, still somewhat in shock. "What in God's name are you doing here?"

"It's a long story—but trust me, God's got nothing to do with it."

I looked to Theo and realized an introduction was in order. "Theo Thompson, this is Sandra Faraday."

"You just saved our lives," he stammered.

"Don't be too quick to thank me, kid. We're not out of the woods yet." Sandra turned her attention to Sheriff Hill who was rubbing his eyes and forehead. "How about you, Sheriff?"

"I'm fine," he replied, "just a little dazed." The sheriff took notice of Sandra's weapon and a look of concern swept over his face. "Where'd you get the sword from?"

Sandra slung the medieval blade over her shoulder and declared, "I took it out of the door upstairs, right before I sealed it shut behind me."

"What?" Theo exclaimed, aghast and enraged by her bold confession. "We're locked inside this tomb? No one knows we're down here."

"Don't worry," Sandra assured him, "I grabbed the key. We can open the door from this side if we survive long enough to make it back there. If not, no one will ever open that door again."

"What are you saying?" I asked.

"I'm sorry, Pam, but you didn't listen when I tried to stop you. Now it's too late to turn back. If we don't succeed down here, we have to make sure that this thing is contained. We can't let it loose and we can't allow anyone else to find their way down here."

"Are you insane?" The sheriff's voice boomed with anger, echoing throughout the stone crypt. "There's some kind of demonic spirit loose in this house and you just trapped us in its lair?"

"Maybe that was her plan." Theo nodded his head toward Sandra. "Think about it. She could have been lying all along. What if she's part of this black magic cult? Maybe she arranged for the accident that killed those two investigators. What if she came back here when my friends were in the house? She's the one who told you the stories about Belladonna and what happened to my friends. Maybe she's responsible for all of this."

"You're just full of wild conspiracy theories, aren't you, kid?" Sandra retorted. There were notes of disgust and sadness in her voice. "Well, here's another one for you. Maybe it was you. You could have made your father swerve his car into that tree. You could have followed your friends into the house and made sure they would never come back out. Maybe it was your plan to lure us into this hellhole."

Before Theo could answer her charges, Sandra shifted her accusations toward the sheriff. "And how about you, Sheriff? You're the one with the key to the front door, and the key to the cellar, yet you never checked down here, not even after those kids went missing?"

"The door was locked," he snapped back, "and as far as I knew, they didn't have any way to open it."

"Listen to us!" I shouted. "We're turning on each other. That's exactly what it wants. That's what it feeds off of—hatred and fear, human suffering and misery. That's why it won't let the spirits of the dead rest. It's still feeding off of them. Feeding off of their eternal torment. It's ancient and undying. It's evil—pure evil in its blackest form, and it has us right where it wants us. If we die here, our souls will never escape. We'll spend the rest of eternity trapped in this hell."

Sheriff Hill drew in a deep breath, allowing the frigid air to cool his temper. "She's right," he said. "We've got to stick together if we want to survive."

I turned to Sandra and asked, "So what are we dealing with here?"

Sandra set her sword down, resting it against a sealed tomb engraved with the name of Edmund Darklore. "Some ancient legends refer to the Devil as the Master of Lies and say that he can appear in any form. The Brotherhood worshiped something called Thule, but Belladonna's spirit called it the Sandman. I think this thing manifests our dreams and nightmares. It waits until you're most vulnerable then deceives you into thinking that it's whatever god you pray to. I suspect it manipulated all of them into doing its bidding."

Sandra looked around the crypt, seemingly searching for some hidden key to unlocking the mystery of the Darklore curse until at last her eyes came to rest on the ritual dagger that Belladonna held. Before anyone could object, she approached the black altar and pried the dagger from the corpse's hands then clasped it tightly in her own. Sandra closed her eyes as she attempted to tap into the memories locked within the bloodstained blade, and as the past revealed itself to her, she began to relate a macabre tale.

"It began long ago—long before the mansion was ever built. Edmund Darklore had heard the stories of the Gloucester region and believed that the land held mystical powers. After surveying the territory and researching its history, he built his home at the epicenter of the forest's spiritual energy. He and the town elders founded a secret brotherhood known as the Knights of Thule and they conducted their clandestine meetings here in this subterranean vault. Each of the thirteen members received a key to the chamber door.

"On the eve of each new moon, the Knights of Thule gathered to perform long-forgotten rituals, reciting incantations from forbidden texts and ancient scrolls. Their arcane rites awakened one of the banished lords of darkness, who silently watched and waited, biding its time before making its presence known to them. When the entity made contact with them, it led them to believe they were telepathically communicating with Thule, an ancient deity, worshiped by the brotherhood. The deception worked, and the sinister spirit began to use the cult's own beliefs against them in an attempt to get them to do its bidding. Allowing them to believe what they wanted, the ancient spirit demanded a sacrifice of blood. They slaughtered a goat, and it appeased the dark one's sanguine thirst, but soon it demanded a human sacrifice. Edmund Darklore refused and sealed the chamber, disbanding the Knights of Thule and forbidding anyone from entering the crypt.

"Years later, when Edmund died, his son Damon inherited the mansion and its macabre secrets. Although it had been strictly forbidden, he reopened the crypt and reinstated the dark Brotherhood of Thule. Damon soon became fixated upon his occult activities and his arcane obsession caused him to ignore his family.

"Neglected by her father, Damon's young daughter, Belladonna, found solace in an unseen friend who whispered to her each night as she lay in bed, filling her young head with twisted thoughts. She recited a nursery rhyme to summon him and the dark entity visited her in her dreams. In the guise of the consoling Sandman, the beguiling spirit played upon her weaknesses and quickly gained her trust. In time, it turned the young girl against her father and convinced her that the members of the Brotherhood were sinners who must be punished for their heathen practices.

"Once again, the dark one demanded a blood sacrifice in the ritual chamber. Belladonna stole her father's key and snuck down into the family crypt. Her mother, Elizabeth, followed her and caught her in the act of spilling her own blood. At the Sandman's instruction, Belladonna had sliced open her left palm and was allowing the blood to flow into the ceremonial chalice as it rested on the altar. Her mother screamed and ran to stop her, causing the startled girl to spin toward her with the dagger in her hand. The silver blade punctured Elizabeth's heart, killing her instantly and bathing Belladonna in her mother's blood."

Sandra took a deep breath, considering the dagger in her hands as the tarnished blade reflected the sheriff's flashlight beam.

"Alerted by Elizabeth's scream," Sandra continued, "Damon rushed down into the crypt, arriving to find Belladonna holding the bloodstained dagger over his wife's dead body. Confronted by the horrific truth, Damon tried to save his daughter from the vile force that had corrupted her innocent soul. Fearing that the girl was possessed, Damon attempted to exorcise the demon.

"As he chanted the rite of exorcism, strange shadows began to rise from the spot where Elizabeth's blood had seeped into the earth. Oily black tentacles reached out of the ground, encircling Belladonna as she lay helpless upon the interment altar. The shadows took hold, and as they wrapped themselves around the girl's body, her pale flesh began to blister and shrivel from their poisonous touch. Belladonna screamed as the darkness took hold of her soul. Within seconds the beautiful girl was reduced to a withered heap of smoldering flesh and bone before her father's eyes.

"The heavy granite door slammed shut, sealing Damon inside the chamber. He whirled around to see a tall shadow in the shape of a man towering over him. The shadow grabbed Damon by the throat and its clawed fingertips began to glow like red-hot irons in a molten fire. The fiendish entity drove the scorching spikes into Damon's eyes, viciously blinding him and cruelly leaving him alive so that his last memory of sight was the grisly vision of his dead wife and daughter. Realizing his horrible fate, Damon vowed that the dark spirit would never escape the tomb. In his last moments his fumbling hands found the sacrificial chalice and he used Belladonna's blood to scrawl a glyph of binding on the inside of the tomb door, sealing the chamber and trapping the beast inside the Darklore crypt.

"Imprisoned by the spell, the entity remained entombed inside the burial vault until Andrea Mather's incantation unknowingly released it by dispersing the ward. Resurrected and summoned forth from the tomb, the dark one now lurks amidst the unholy shadows of Darklore Manor."

Sandra finished her macabre tale and looked down at the corpses strewn in tortured poses on the crypt floor. A tarnished chalice rested beside the skeletal remains of Damon Darklore.

Theo's voice trembled as he assessed our grim situation. "If what you say is true, then we're trapped like rats in a cage. There's no way that thing will ever let us leave this place. We'll die in this crypt and no one will ever know we're down her."

Sandra cast her gaze upon the mystic sigil on the tomb door, intently studying the bloodstained glyph. "I don't think it will risk entering the crypt and getting trapped in here again."

"What good does that do us?"?Theo asked. "There's only one way out of here. We'll be dead as soon as we step outside that door."

The sheriff withdrew his revolver. "We can't cower in here forever. If we're going to die, I'm not going down without a fight."

Sandra shook her head. "I'm afraid bullets won't have any effect on this thing. But you're right, we can't stay here very long."

"Why not?" Theo asked.

"You saw how it brought that doll to life." Sandra motioned her head toward the shattered remains of the sinister toy. "If it can possess inanimate objects, then I suspect it has the ability to control the dead and manipulate them like puppets."

Theo cautiously backed away from the corpses that lay at his feet, joining the sheriff and myself inside the lantern's dim halo.

"It sounds like we're damned either way," Sheriff Hill said, shifting his gaze between Belladonna's body and the doorway.

"No," Sandra replied, "I think there's a way we can send this thing back to whatever hell it came from, but you're going to have to trust me."

"What's your plan?" the sheriff asked.

Sandra's reply quashed what little shred of hope I had been clinging to. "We have to unleash our worst fears."

"What?" I gasped. "That's exactly what this thing wants."

"I know," Sandra said, looking me directly in the eye. "Like I said, you're going to have to trust me."

The sheriff clenched his jaw as he pondered our seemingly hopeless situation, then growled, "What other choice do we have?"

Sandra picked up the chalice that lay on the floor, then stepped to the altar and set the tarnished goblet down beside Belladonna's remains. She lifted the ceremonial dagger and grasped the blade tightly in her left hand then closed her eyes and yanked the knife across her palm, slicing it wide open. I shuddered as I watched a stream of crimson run down her frail wrist. Sandra held her palm over the chalice and let her blood drip into it until the goblet was nearly half-full, then she removed a silk scarf and wrapped it around her hand to bandage the gaping wound. She slipped the dagger beneath her jacket and into her belt then carefully lifted the chalice and stepped toward the exit.

"Let's go," she said. "Stay close behind me. When we get to the ritual chamber, follow my lead, but whatever you do, don't say a word."

Sandra led us out into the mist-shrouded corridor and as we

left the sanctity of the crypt I began to get the sickening feeling that we had made a terrible mistake. Though Sandra's knowledge of the occult was unparalleled, a part of me wondered if her mind hadn't been twisted by her numerous dalliances with the dark side. The eccentric woman who was leading us into a deadly confrontation with the forces of darkness was an unpredictable stranger who bore little resemblance to the stable-minded professional that I had once known. I did not doubt that she would give her own life to save the souls of those who had died here, but I feared she might sacrifice us all, if need be, in order to vanquish the infernal entity that haunted Darklore Manor. Even though I had begun to question her sanity, I realized that our only hope for survival lay in trusting her.

As we proceeded along the corridor toward the ritual chamber chattering whispers echoed from the darkness ahead. A freezing chill descended upon us as we entered the pitch black room. Grim specters of the restless dead emerged from the shadows and began to close in. The ghostly silhouettes ambled forth in a shuffling gait to surround us on all sides. Their skeletal faces were twisted into inhuman masks that stared at us with soulless eyes. Sandra held the bloody chalice high above her head and the shadows recoiled, allowing us passage between their nightmarish ranks.

Sandra continued forward until she reached the middle of the room then stopped before the ritual circle that was inscribed on the floor beside the altar. She removed the goat skull from the ancient tabernacle and set it on the ground in the center of the circle. A ghostly moan began to rise, as if her actions had awakened an ancient immortal spirit from its eternal slumber. Sandra quickly lit the three black candles that surrounded the ritual circle, then dipped her fingers into the chalice and used her blood to trace a large triangle between them. Strange voices whispered while other unearthly sounds screeched and chattered from the shadows around us.

Sandra held forth the chalice and began to recite an unholy

incantation to summon the beast of Darklore Manor from the depths of the abyss. "Hail the Lord of Shadows, bringer of death and eternal torment. We have come to serve thee." Sandra's voice bellowed throughout the chamber. "Reveal to us thy true form, so that we may bow before thy dark majesty. Arise, master, arise!"

We remained petrified as Sandra uttered her blasphemous invocation. An eerie hush fell over the room, plunging the crypt into unnerving silence until the sound of heavy pounding broke the deathly calm. The rhythmic pulse grew louder and louder until the slow drumming of a thunderous heartbeat reverberated throughout the chamber. Then, as if summoned by the ominous sound, a writhing swarm of serpentine shadows rose from the darkness. We watched in horror as the black tentacles crept up the stone walls and slithered across the ceiling to loom menacingly overhead.

Within the ritual circle, worm-like tendrils of black mist emerged from the ground beneath the horned skull to squirm across its pitted surface and entwine themselves around its twisting horns. The wriggling mass of shadows clung to the decayed bone, forming a hideous face, and the skull began to rise up, held aloft by a billowing column of black smoke that issued forth from the ground beneath it.

Sandra stepped to the very edge of the circle and continued her sinister invocation. "We beseech thee, O Lord of Shadows, cast thy fiery gaze upon thy mortal servants. Trample thy enemies beneath thy cloven hooves, yet spare those who are thy humble slaves."

As she spoke, molten red orbs glared from within the skull's empty eye sockets and the billowing cloud began to take on a beastly form. We stood awestruck and horrified as we watched it sprout sinewy arms ending in skeletal hands with razor-sharp claws and long goat-like legs covered in shaggy black fur.

Sandra raised her arms out to her sides. "Spread thy ebon wings to wrap our immortal souls in thy dark embrace."

As the monstrous apparition rose higher, black leathery wings sprouted from the beast's back and stretched outward to span the shadows before us. The demon's features shifted to match each new verse Sandra recited, as if she were somehow sculpting its ungodly semblance with her words. It seemed to be latching onto images from the darkest recesses of our minds and transforming our nightmares into reality.

Sandra's voice reached a crescendo as she made her final decree. "We have shed our life's essence and we offer thee our blood."

The hellish creature stood glowering over us, its eyes seething with unearthly fire. Sandra bowed before the demon, raising the blood-soaked chalice as an offering to the unholy beast that was now living flesh. I stood trembling as I gazed upward—horrified and repulsed by the loathsome abomination that loomed before me. The black beast issued forth a low rumbling growl then threw its horned head back in diabolic rapture.

Sandra quickly took hold of the ceremonial knife that she had tucked in her belt. In one swift motion, she thrust the dagger up into the demon's chest, piercing his black flesh just below the sternum, driving the blade upward into its heart. A terrible roar erupted from the wounded fiend as its black blood spilled to the floor and the walls echoed with the cries of a thousand tormented souls.

*"Run, now!"* Sandra shouted, as she dropped the chalice and bolted for the stairs. "*Go!*"

The monstrous beast flailed and shrieked in agony, but it could not escape the confines of the ritual circle.

*"Don't look back!"* she screamed.

Sandra leapt through the encompassing shadows and hit the cellar stairs running, with the rest of us in frenzied pursuit. The narrow staircase passage forced us to ascend in single file. I was immediately behind Sandra, followed by the sheriff and Theo. I could hear the shrieks and wails of the hellish legions that trailed close behind us, but I dared not look back. I frantically leapt up each step, but as I neared the middle of the staircase I lost my footing in the darkness. I stumbled and fell, blocking the passage for the sheriff and Theo. Without a moment's hesitation, the sheriff scooped me up in his arms and slung me over his shoulder then continued to run up the steps completely undeterred by my added weight.

As I gazed back down the staircase I could see the horrors that had risen from the forsaken crypt. An undulating sea of monstrous forms stretched out of the darkness to thwart our escape. Theo bounded up the stairs only a few steps ahead of the pursuing shadows. Barbed tentacles flailed through the air and loathsome talons clawed the walls behind him.

When we reached the top of the staircase, Sandra hurried to insert the key in the keyhole. I heard the lock turn and the squeal of hinges, followed by an eerie moment of silence. Time seemed to stand still and each second hung in the air like an eternity. From somewhere in the darkness behind us, a soft voice called Theo's name. He turned to heed the hypnotic call and his gaze was met by a familiar face. The spectral form of Andrea Mather was standing on the staircase behind him.

"Theo," she whispered.

"Andrea?"

"Don't leave us here, Theo," her soft voice pleaded. She stretched her pale arms out toward him and Theo reached back to take her hand.

*"No, Theo!"* I screamed. But my warning was too late.

The instant he took hold of her hand, Andrea's form deteriorated into the withered corpse of Belladonna. A legion of hellish shadows swarmed over him and within seconds he was covered in oily black tentacles. A taloned hand reached out from the shadowy blackness. Theo struggled to escape its grasp but its ebon claws stretched over the top of his head, digging its monstrous nails into his flesh. With a violent crack, the shadow snapped Theo's neck, twisting his head around to face the opposite direction. Dark blood spurted from his lips and his eyes stared in horror as his body was dragged back down the staircase and swallowed by the infernal blackness of the crypt below.

*"NO!"* I cried out. But I had no time to grieve.

Belladonna's ghastly corpse continued to ascend the staircase, closing the short distance between us. Behind her, coiled tentacles slithered forth, stretching upward along the mossy stone walls. The sheriff lunged forward up the last few steps and through the library door. As soon as my head cleared the exit, Sandra slammed the door closed and twisted the key in the lock. Inhuman shrieks wailed from beyond the sealed barrier, followed by a violent barrage of thunderous pounding that threatened to tear the door from its hinges.

As the infernal shadows continued their furious assault against the locked door Sandra barked, "Stand back!" She tore the wrapping from her wounded hand and smeared her palm across the door, painting the glyph of binding in her own blood.

"Get out of here, now!" the sheriff shouted. "Run!"

We bolted out of the library and down the corridor leading to the entrance hall. The shadows seemed to close in from all sides, constricting our path as we fled for our lives. With bounding leaps we sprinted beneath the towering sentinel knights and out the open door, making our escape from the accursed house that had claimed the lives of so many others.

My heart pounded violently as I reached the lawn and fell to my knees, shuddering and gasping for breath. I broke down in tears as I thought of the horrible fate we had nearly suffered.

Sheriff Hill reached down and gently helped me to my feet. As I stared up at the mansion that loomed in the ghostly mist I felt a strange sense of calm and I realized that I was no longer burdened by the oppressive fear that had plagued my life for the past four years.

Sandra whispered, "We're safe now."

I wiped the tears from my eyes. "You had me scared for a while."

"I'm sorry," she said. "I couldn't explain things down there. I could sense that it was probing our minds and I couldn't risk letting it discover my plan."

The sheriff looked at Sandra curiously, as if he were scrutinizing the validity of her story. "You had me convinced that you were conjuring the Devil himself up from the fiery depths of the abyss."

"I needed to create a mental image that we all could focus on so that the entity would latch onto our thoughts and manifest our fears."

"Why?" Sheriff Hill asked.

"I needed to trick it into assuming a physical form so that I could spill its blood. It was the only component that was powerful enough to contain it and trap it inside the ritual circle."

The sheriff stared at her in disbelief. "You used its own blood against it?"

"Yes," she said. "I remembered what the spirit of Damon Darklore whispered to me when we encountered his ghost during our first investigation. He said that more blood had to be spilled. I originally interpreted it as an ominous threat from beyond the grave, but after I discovered that he was trapped inside the mansion, along with the others that died here, I reasoned that his spirit was trying to tell us how to break the curse and set them free."

"Do you think it's finally over?" I asked.

"I don't know." Sandra shook her head. "Only time will tell."

The sheriff cast a hard look toward the mansion as if he were staring down a mortal enemy.

"What about Theo?"?I asked.

The sheriff hung his head. "He's been in and out of foster homes since he was six. He's run away from every one of them. Someone's bound to file a missing person's report, but I doubt anyone will think that his disappearance is unusual. His life ended ten years ago when that thing stole his parents. The memories tormented him and filled his heart with hatred. Vengeance was the only thing that kept him going after his friends died, but it clouded his vision. In the end it consumed him."

"He was the last in the bloodline of the Knights of Thule," Sandra said. "It wanted him most of all."

"So what do we do now?" I asked.

The sheriff sighed. "Nothing we say could ever convince people to stay clear of this place. Who would believe us?" He walked to his patrol car, opened the trunk and pulled out a can of gasoline.

I stared in disbelief as he carried the can back to the mansion's porch. "What are you doing?"

"Something I should have done a long time ago. If I had, that kid would still be alive. By my count, seventeen people have died here. That thing inside killed them. I'm not going to have any more deaths on my conscience. I'm making sure it doesn't happen again—not on my watch."

He splashed the gas over the entrance door, emptying the contents of the can onto the front of the house, then lit a match and tossed it onto the porch. Within minutes, the old house had erupted into flames. Writhing tendrils of fire snaked outward and upward, reminding all of us of the tentacled demon entombed in the Darklore crypt. The three of us stood transfixed by the inferno before us as if we were gazing into the fires of Hell itself.

After a long moment of silence I asked, "What about their bodies? They deserve a proper burial."

"We can't afford to excavate this ground," Sandra said coldly. "If we didn't kill that thing, at least it's trapped down there."

"It's better we leave our secrets buried," the sheriff said solemnly. "Ashes to ashes, and dust to dust."

"Dust... and shadows," Sandra whispered.

On Halloween night in 1971, Darklore Manor was the scene of a mysterious fire, and the mansion burned to the ground. The official police report lists the cause of the fire as arson. However, there are rumors of a cover-up concerning certain facts of the investigation, including the discovery of skeletal remains of several bodies found deep in the foundation of the charred ruins.

Six months after the mansion was razed, Sheriff George Hill suffered a fatal heart attack and died in his sleep. Four years later, Sandra Faraday went missing under mysterious circumstances. Her whereabouts remain unknown to this day, but rumors claim that she was driven mad by what she saw inside Darklore Manor and was committed to an asylum. Others say that she took her own life. Whatever the case, I alone am the last to know of the horrors that dwelled within that accursed place, and I feel a deep obligation to share the truth with those who might gain from it.

I have often thought of what I encountered inside Darklore Manor. Occasionally the nightmares return and the visions of Belladonna, the shadow man and the diabolical doll still haunt me. But I find solace in the fact that my dreams are merely the remnants of distant memories from a time long past when I was enslaved by my fears.

There are many people who have explored the fringes of the shadow domain and glimpsed vestiges of the unseen world that surrounds us. Many of us know that there are portals to the spiritual plane that can be breached, allowing the dead to trespass upon the realm of the living. And though this ultimate knowledge offers proof of life beyond death, it paints a grim portrait of the horrors that await some in the afterlife.

As for Darklore Manor, few traces of the mansion remain, yet reports of the Lady in Black continue to this day near the site of the old manor house. There are those who say that her wandering spirit is cursed to roam the grounds for eternity as punishment for her mortal sins, and local tales say that her mournful wail can be heard on moonless nights during the midnight hour. Other ghosts are said to haunt the site as well, and although the mansion has been gone for nearly forty years, people continue to avoid the area. For, as I well know, it is a place where spirits of the dead do not rest easy, nor do they find release from their eternal sorrow.

# BORN OF THE NIGHT

## THE GOTHIC FANTASY ARTWORK OF JOSEPH VARGO

*This extensive art collection features over 100 of Vargo's most popular works of gothic fantasy, as well as some rare paintings, drawings and sketches published together for the first time. With an introduction and commentaries by Joseph Iorillo, this volume also offers comprehensive insights into Vargo's gothic domain.*

BORN OF THE NIGHT

THE GOTHIC FANTASY ARTWORK OF
JOSEPH VARGO

*The powerful and captivating artwork of Joseph Vargo opens a gateway to the darkside and dares the viewer to venture within. While his work is dominated by an immense and memorable array of ominous and often nightmarish entities, his timeless images are also permeated with tremendous beauty, grace and symmetry. His art has achieved a resonance and popularity partially because of this ability to shed light on the inner demons that lurk in the shadows of the mind, while also not forgetting the sometimes majestic grandeur that resides there as well. Enter the world of this modern master of the macabre.*

*ISBN 0967575664 Price: $25.00*
*100 color plates, 40 b+w illustrations, 184 pages.*

AVAILABLE AT
MONOLITHGRAPHICS.COM
AND AMAZON.COM